Teach Me to Fly Skyfighter!

AND OTHER STORIES

To Jamie,
welcome to my neighbourhood!

happy reading!

Paul Yee

PAUL YEE

Teach Me to Fly, Skyfighter!

AND OTHER STORIES

Illustrated by Sky Lee

James Lorimer & Company, Publishers
Toronto 1983

Canadian Cataloguing in Publication Data

Yee, Paul.
Teach me to fly, Skyfighter!

(The Adventure in Canada Series)
ISBN 0-88862-646-0 (bound). — ISBN 0-88862-645-2 (pbk).
1. Chinese Canadians —Juvenile fiction.* I. Title.II. Series.

PS8597.E3T32   jc813'.54   C83-098298-1
PZ7.Y43Te

This book was published with the support of the Multicultural
Program, Government of Canada.

Design: Michael Solomon

Teacher's guide available from the publisher.
Write to the address below.

The Adventure in Canada Series
James Lorimer & Company, Publishers
Egerton Ryerson Memorial Building
35 Britain Street
Toronto, M5A IR7, Ontario

Printed and bound in Canada

The author wishes to thank the following people for their assistance in the development of this book: Doris Cowan, Nancy Masters, Rick Coe, Rowly Lorimer, Jim Gaskell, Hayne Wai, Jim Wong-Chu, Selina Chew, Sharon Lee, Judy Chan, Gayle Chin, Stratheona Community Centre staff members Wendy Au and Greg Eng, and Strathcona Elementary School teachers Dan Mcdougall, Glenn Nagano and Wally Ng.

Contents

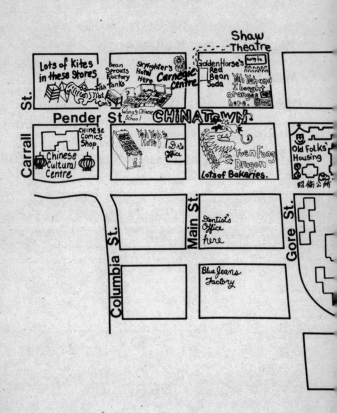

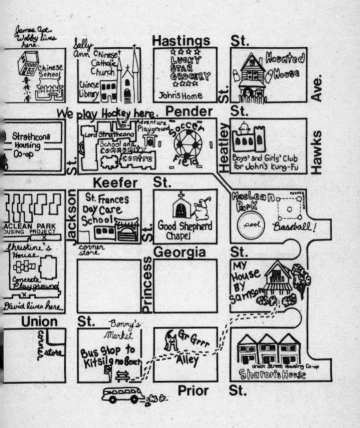

Teach Me to Fly, Skyfighter!

Teach Me to Fly, Skyfighter!

SHARON Fong felt hot and angry, and it wasn't from the bright afternoon sun pouring down on her. It had been a rainy summer in Vancouver, so Sharon really enjoyed the little sunshine that occasionally broke through. It was Samson Wong, the shrimpy loudmouth from their grade five class, who was ruining her day. Sharon knew that Samson was the fastest forward on their hockey team, the Dragons, but when he found an audience for himself he could be a real pain.

The kids hanging around the front of the Strathcona Community Centre had clustered around Samson as soon as he appeared. He had brought a huge kite with him. It was shaped like a butterfly, with long cellophane streamers that sparkled in the sunshine. All of Samson's friends had started to laugh and shout in Chinese. Sharon hated it when Samson and the immigrant kids used Chinese. They spoke too fast and used words she didn't know. Sometimes she was sure they were laughing and talking about her. Sharon understood Chinese only when it was spoken slowly, and she didn't like speaking it herself. So now she tried her best to ignore them.

She stared down past her long brown legs at her dusty sandals, and then she looked across the parking lot to Pender Street. Cars were parked everywhere: alongside the school next door, by the church with its fancy pointed spires, and in front of all the houses and their neat little gardens. Pender Street was always crowded because it led straight into Chinatown, three blocks away. Chinatown, with its busy stores, restaurants, theatres, and bakeries, attracted people from all over Vancouver to the neighbourhood.

Sharon would never have admitted it aloud, but she disliked Chinatown. Everyone shopping there spoke Chinese, and at the top of their lungs, it seemed. She was never sure what was being said. The storekeepers set bins of fruits and vegetables out on the sidewalk, and it was hard to move quickly through the crowds. Being surrounded by Chinese people made Sharon uncomfortable because she did not feel very Chinese herself. She did not feel that she belonged here at all.

Sharon's family had moved into Strathcona six months ago from Vancouver Island. Her parents wanted to be near her grandfather, who lived alone in Chinatown. Sharon had not been happy about the move. Their old house had been big and roomy, with shady trees to climb in the front and back yards. Now the Fongs lived in co-op housing, where several townhouse families shared garden and yard space. There was only one bathroom in their new place, and Sharon's room was a lot smaller. But there was another reason for Sharon's unhappiness. The big problem was that almost everyone in her class was Chinese.

Sharon had known other Chinese kids, like her cousins and old friends on the Island. But they had been just like her, Canadian-born and English-speaking. They would tell jokes, fool around, and act just like their white friends.

In Strathcona, there were a lot of recent immigrant kids from Hong Kong and China. They were shy and clumsy, spoke broken English, and wore the funniest-looking clothes. Some even brought rice from home, in thermos bottles, to eat in the school cafeteria at lunch. Sharon realized that she looked like just another Chinese, but she was determined to show everyone that she was different.

Sharon was already one of the tallest girls in the class, and she kept her shiny hair cut short, in a smooth, neat, grown-up style. Her face and arms

4

were tanned coconut-brown from playing outside all the time. She spoke up frequently in class, and played hockey on the Dragons team every day after school. But Sharon still felt uneasy. She wasn't sure if it was because she was still new to the neighbourhood, or if it was because she wasn't sure what to do about being Chinese.

Summer had finally arrived. School was finished, but Sharon still saw the other Dragons every day. Samson, John, Christine, and Man-Chok were all enrolled in the Summer Fun program at the community centre. In their spare time, all the kids in the area hung around the centre, which had a gym, a crafts room, a library, and a games room with a big green billiards table in it. The centre was busy all day long, with classes for adults and programs for senior citizens, the handicapped, and new immigrants.

The parents of Strathcona were thankful for the summer program, because most of them had to work and could not look after their children all day. Some kids tried to earn money picking strawberries at a farm, but the rains had ruined this year's crop. The summer program was lots more fun than school, since there was no homework. The kids had visited museums and factories, gone hiking and swimming, and tried different crafts. Next week, they were going kite-flying at the beach down at Kitsilano Park.

When Jane, their group leader, had announced the trip last week, the kids had responded with a great shout of excitement. It would be a real treat to go to the beach, just half an hour's bus-ride away. Sharon had seen kites on TV, but she had never flown one herself. Neither had anyone else in the group. Not everyone could afford to buy a kite, so Jane said she would bring some frisbees and a few extra kites.

Sharon was lucky, even though she had already spent her allowance money. Her brother Eddy had bought a kite at last summer's Japanese festival at nearby Oppenheimer Park. It was simply designed, with a large square of brightly painted rice paper on a slender frame. Eddy had never found time to fly it, so Sharon would be the first to try it out. Today, some kids had brought their kites to show Jane, in hopes that she would take them flying, but there wasn't enough wind. And anyway, Jane couldn't get away.

Suddenly, Samson was speaking English. Sharon looked up. He was showing the kite to Christine, who had just arrived. Chris stood almost a full head taller than Samson, and her face was covered with freckles. She was wearing her usual T-shirt, blue jeans and sneakers.

"We must have used ten metres of bamboo, and I got to cut them and shape them!" Samson's scratchy voice became louder. "My dad had these stiletto blades so sharp they could slice through your thumb without you feeling anything!"

"Oh, yeah, really?" Chris tried to look impressed and serious for Samson, and then she grinned over at Sharon. Sharon shook her head. Chris was one of her best friends, and today she seemed to be in a good mood, because she was usually not so friendly and chatty. But still, she could play at being too nice to Samson. Sharon could never bring herself to say anything nice to him, that was for sure.

Samson, not noticing the look the girls exchanged, went on bragging about his kite. "So I had my dad make the wings extra big so that it'll fly extra high. We were going to try it out yesterday, only it rained."

Chris came to sit by Sharon while the others picked up in Chinese again. "This is your kite, eh?" Chris picked up Sharon's square. "Did you make it yourself?"

"Nah." Sharon shrugged and tried to sound casual. "Didn't have any time." She made a face at

7

Samson's crowd. "Jeez, I don't know what they're so excited about." It really embarrassed Sharon when they spoke Chinese in front of Chris, or anyone who was not Chinese.

"Yeah, it's just a bunch of sticks and paper glued together," Chris said lazily, squinting into the fierce sunlight. She poked her chin out at Samson. "What's he saying, anyway?"

"Who cares?" answered Sharon. "He's just talking big." But deep down inside her, Sharon did care. She had wished many times that she knew better Chinese. Then Samson wouldn't have anything over her. Then she could fit in and still be different.

Chris was leaning back with a faraway look in her eyes. "You know what I think we should do?" she asked. "Rent roller skates and go around the seawall!"

"Hey, we should! That would be fun!" And they started to plan it out. Then Sharon heard the kids break out in a fresh round of laughter. Samson was laughing so hard that he was bent double. And they were pointing at her kite. Samson had probably made an obscene comment about it, Sharon thought.

"What's so funny?" she demanded.

"Nothing." Samson was trying to look innocent, but his mouth twitched and he turned his head away.

"Then how come you're laughing so hard? Trying to ruin your health?" Sharon felt like grabbing him and shaking him until his teeth rattled. But then they would probably call her a bully for picking on someone smaller.

Samson said something fast in Chinese, and his friends burst out laughing. "Hey, Sharon, come on. Can't you take a joke?" asked Samson, noticing the scowl on Sharon's face.

"Depends." Sharon got up and hooked her thumbs into her belt loops. "Why don't you speak English? This is Canada, you know." Even as Sharon said this, she regretted it.

But Samson shrugged and made another quick remark that set his audience off hooting again. Sharon lunged, grabbing at Samson's kite, but he quickly jerked it away.

"Hey, you!" he taunted. "Hands off! This is valuable property!"

"It's a pile of junk!" Sharon retorted.

"You should talk," sneered Samson. "Look at yours, it doesn't even have wings. It's square like you, you blockhead!"

"Don't you worry. It'll fly. It'll go higher than yours!"

"Oh, yeah?" Samson's grin stretched from ear to ear. "It'll be like watching a cow try to fly!"

Sharon jumped for Samson this time, but at that moment, Jane opened the door. "Hey, what's going on?" she asked.

"Nothing, nothing." The kids dispersed in a million directions, and Sharon headed home. But all she could see was Samson's smirking face. Sharon wanted desperately to show Samson and all his immigrant friends that they couldn't laugh at her just because she didn't speak Chinese. She would show him, once and for all. But how? Sharon didn't know what to do.

When Sharon walked in the front door at home, she groaned inwardly. This was not her day. Her grandfather was visiting, carrying his smelly tobacco pipe, and wearing his baggy but neatly creased pants and polished black shoes. Sharon called him *Yeh-yeh*, the Chinese word for grandfather. He was a tall, slim gentleman, with skin that had darkened and loosened with age. He sat in the Fongs' living room, watching TV. He looked up and a smile lit his face.

10

"Back home from school, Ying?" he asked. "Ying" was part of Sharon's Chinese name, but Yeh-yeh was the only person who ever used it.

Sharon nodded and dashed upstairs to her room. She threw the kite on the floor and flung herself down on her bed. Boy, did that Samson ever make her mad. She was sick of his bragging and his Chinese double-talk. Now it looked as if they were going to fight it out with kites. But Sharon was far from sure she had a chance of winning. Her kite didn't have wings, it had never been flown, and she didn't have time to test it out anywhere close by. She could feel her resentment about immigrants rise up inside her as she stared angrily at the ceiling.

Samson was the one who made her feel most like an outsider. He could play hockey and speak up just as well as Sharon could. Sharon could hear that his English wasn't absolutely perfect, but Samson was more than happy with it. Mostly, it was Samson's being so comfortable, so relaxed about being Chinese that bothered her. Sharon refused to believe that just being able to speak Chinese made all the difference. She was jealous of Samson, but she wasn't sure why; she didn't want to be like him. And she had no idea how she was going to fly a better kite than his.

11

Finally she got up and went downstairs. May as well watch some TV, she thought. Things can't get worse today.

In the tiny living room, Yeh-yeh sat straight and erect, and gazed at the TV with alert eyes. Sharon usually draped herself comfortably all over the sofa to watch TV, but today she sat on the floor away from Yeh-yeh. She thought he had a peculiar smell around him. She went to the window, where the sill was covered with her mother's potted plants, to let in some fresh air.

The two of them sat for a while without saying anything. Yeh-yeh had spent most of his life in Canada, and understood English better than he spoke it. It was almost the same situation with Sharon's Chinese. Sharon thought the game show on TV was dumb, but Yeh-yeh seemed to enjoy it as he laughed and groaned with the contestants. Then he reached into his pocket and pulled out a package.

"Do you want some candy?" he asked, holding out a handful of Smarties. Sharon looked greedily at the coloured chocolates for a moment, but shook her head. She could not bring herself to eat anything he had touched. It was all because of that last time she had visited him.

Yeh-yeh lived in an old hotel in Chinatown. There was a busy restaurant at street level, and long narrow stairs led to the rooms above. It was like stepping into a different world because while the street was crowded and bustling, the upstairs was cool and quiet with corridors that melted into the dark.

Yeh-yeh's dingy little room had a bed, a wooden table, two rickety chairs, and cardboard boxes piled into the corner. A TV set rested on top of an old trunk beside a clutter of family photographs. The tiny window overlooked the alley, where hot greasy odours from the restaurant lingered.

On Sharon's last visit, Yeh-yeh had bought some hot Chinese buns at a bakery, and he made tea while Sharon sat waiting. They were in the communal kitchen that Yeh-yeh shared with nine other men living on his floor. Suddenly a shiny brown bug darted out from under the bag and sprinted across the table. Sharon screamed and jumped away. Yeh-yeh swore softly and said, "Cockroaches again!"

Ever since that day, Sharon had been afraid to visit Yeh-yeh. How could anyone live with cockroaches in their kitchen? She had wondered if all the other old men hanging around Chinatown

13

lived like that and had shuddered. Grandfather was like Samson, they both reminded Sharon that she looked Chinese on the outside, but did not feel Chinese inside. Her Chinese self, the part of her that was the child of Chinese parents, seemed far away — too remote to mean anything. Sharon was Canadian, and that was what she wanted to be.

Then she heard her mother's voice. "Sharon, come set the table," she called from the kitchen.

At dinner, everyone looked tired. Sharon's mom had missed her lunch because the office had been extra busy. Eddy was feeling stiff and sore after another day with the road-paving crew. He was a university student, but worked during the summer to pay his tuition. And Sharon's dad could hardly wait for his weekend off from the furniture factory. Nobody noticed that Sharon was quieter than usual.

Sharon's mom started talking to Yeh-yeh about moving in with them. She said it would be easier for him. He wouldn't have so many stairs to climb. Sharon did not pay much attention because she had heard this conversation many times before. Yeh-yeh always refused, and said that he was used to being alone. After so many years, he liked the independence, and the peace and quiet.

Eddy took a loud slurp of soup and put his bowl down. He was the fastest eater at the table and always finished first. Mom had nicknamed him "hog."

"How's the kite, kiddo?" he asked.

Sharon snapped at him, "Don't call me kiddo! You hog!" Then she announced, "I think it's going to flop. It doesn't have any wings."

"Kites don't need wings to fly," he answered.

"Well, you should see Samson's. His is like a butterfly, with four huge wings." Sharon began to pout. "He's going to make me look like a fool … " She turned to her father and asked, "Dad, do you know how to build kites?"

He shook his head. "No, I don't. How about you, Ba?" he asked Yeh-yeh, mixing the Chinese word for father with his English.

Yeh-yeh also shook his head. "Me, I've never made one." He paused. "But I remember seeing kites. When I was small, there were kites built like eagles and hawks, and even one built like a dragon."

"You had kites when you were small?" asked Sharon in surprise. She had never thought of her Yeh-yeh being a kid and playing games.

"Sure he did," interrupted Eddy with his know-it-all voice. "Didn't you know that the Chinese invented the kite?"

Sharon's father explained that in ancient China, kites had been used by armies to give signals. Different coloured kites were flown to tell armies to attack or to move into different positions. Later, kitefighting became a popular sport among the common people. The kite-fighters coated their lines with tiny bits of glass and sand, and then tried to cut each other's kites loose in the wind.

That's exactly what I'd like to do to Samson! Sharon thought. Her mother began to clear away the dishes. Sharon usually helped, but tonight she was busy listening to Yeh-yeh.

"There's a fellow I knew on the Island," said Yeh-yeh as he filled his pipe. "The men at the mill called him *Teen-jung* Tom, Skyfighter Tom. He was famous for his kites. He built his own and flew them down by the ocean. You should have seen them, they made the eyes ache!" Yeh-yeh lit his pipe and took a long puff, "The men thought he was crazy, always playing with his toys. But I tell you, he's lived longer than any of those who were laughing!"

"Does he still build kites?" Sharon asked eagerly. "I'm not sure," said Yeh-yeh thoughtfully.

"He lives close by, but I haven't seen him lately. I often wonder how he is."

"Why don't you and Yeh-yeh go visit him?" suggested Eddy.

Yeh-yeh thought it was a good idea, but Sharon hesitated. The thought of cockroaches running across dark hallways terrified her.

"What's the matter?" grinned Eddy, as if he had read her mind. "Something bugging you?"

Sharon looked up. "No, nothing bugs me," she declared, setting her chin and saying the word *bugs* loudly. "We'll go tomorrow."

Next day, Sharon found herself wondering if she had made the right decision. She clenched her sweaty hands and listened to her heart pound loudly as she followed Yeh-yeh up the creaky stairs of a Pender Street rooming house. She reminded herself not to scream or jump at the sight of any insect. Her mom had told her to buy some oranges in Chinatown to bring to Skyfighter. It was Chinese good manners, her mom said. Sharon was also told to call Skyfighter *dai-bahk*, which meant great-uncle.

The linoleum in the hallway was bumpy and cracked. A sharp smell of chlorine hung everywhere. Sharon followed her grandfather closely, counting off the room numbers one by one. They stopped before number nine, and Yeh-yeh knocked loudly. After a while, the door opened, and a deep voice sang out in Chinese, "Charlie, it's you! Its been a long time! Come in, come in!"

With a broad smile on his face, Skyfighter moved aside to let Yeh-yeh and Sharon file into his room. Skyfighter's back was bent forward and his face and hands were speckled with dark spots. His shirt and pants seemed a bit big for him. His room was just like Yeh-yeh's, with its few sticks of furniture and a lonely window in the corner. One whole wall was covered with calendars from Chinatown stores, with pretty girls and bright landscapes printed on them. Sharon noticed that some of them were several years old.

Skyfighter followed them stiffly, dragging his feet heavily across the floor. "Sit down, sit down!" he said.

"So, Tom, you're well these days?" asked Yeh-yeh, in the old village dialect.

Skyfighter sighed as he sat down slowly. "As things go, Charlie, pretty good. I wish I were as healthy as you."

Yeh-yeh laughed the compliment away. "Ah, we're all in the same boat, we old-timers. This is my granddaughter, Kwun-ying. Her English name is Sharon."

Sharon swallowed quickly and spoke up loudly. "Hello, Dai- bahk. Here are some oranges for you."

"You didn't have to bring anything," exclaimed Skyfighter as he warmly accepted the fruit. "You don't have to be formal with me. We're all old friends!"

Yeh-yeh sat himself down at the table and picked up the newspaper lying there. "Hmm," he said as he pulled out his reading glasses. "You're a fast one today, Tom. You've already picked up today's edition. Let's see what's new in the world."

"Not much good news," Skyfighter remarked drily as he sat down on his bed. He smoothed out the blanket, and motioned for Sharon to sit down too. From behind the newspaper, Yeh-yeh spoke up in sudden recollection that Sharon was still in the room.

"Tom, Ying here wants to know about your kites," he said absently.

"Oh?" Skyfighter's gaze swivelled to settle on Sharon, who was waiting anxiously. She wasn't sure what to say or do next.

Skyfighter looked at her intently. "So you've heard about my kites."

"Yes, and I ... I'd like to see them," stammered Sharon.

"See them? Why?"

"Because ... because ... " Sharon groped clumsily for Chinese words in a panic. "Because Yeh-yeh said they made the eyes ache!"

"You don't speak Chinese, eh?" Skyfighter pondered that for a moment. Sharon's stomach went queasy, but then Skyfighter started to speak a rough and ragged English. "You salmon-cans are like that — shiny on the outside, but nothing inside!" Then he chuckled to himself and Yeh-yeh made some sounds of agreement from behind his newspaper. "Nothing we can do about that now, is there? You go to Chinese school?"

Sharon nodded, but didn't tell him what a waste of time she thought it was. She also wondered what salmon cans had to do with her. Skyfighter reached down under his bed and pulled out a battered cardboard box. Then he held up a frame of thin bamboo rods lashed together by fine string bindings. Tatters of faded paper dangled here and there. In the dim grey light of the room, it took Sharon a few minutes to make out what it was. Then she saw that it was a hawk, with long wings and broad tail feathers.

When Skyfighter placed the kite in Sharon's hands, she could feel that the frame was light but sturdy as a basket. The tips of each rib had been carefully shaped and joined to fit like pieces of a jigsaw puzzle. The bamboo lengths gleamed as if they had been polished. Sharon had never seen anything so intricately made.

"Wow," she breathed. "It's beautiful! Why don't you fix it up and take it out?"

Skyfighter shook his head slowly, "No, my flying days are all over. When I was a young man, working the shingle mills on the Island, then I flew my kites." He sank comfortably into his chair. "Oh yes, I flew them whenever I had the chance. We didn't have weekends off as you do now."

Skyfighter had lived in a bunk-house with forty other mill-hands — mostly Chinese and Japanese. He told Sharon that he had never been able to bring his wife over to Canada, and his life was very lonely. The other men liked to gamble in their free time, but Skyfighter wanted to save his money. So he started making kites to keep his mind active and to keep from feeling bitter.

"But I had nothing to work with. There were no stores around." Skyfighter's eyes brightened as his memories came alive. "So I picked up my bamboo sleeping mat and ripped it apart, one strip after

21

another. Then I split each one down the middle, and then again. Those were the ribs for the kite frames. I had string, but no glue or paper. So what did I do?"

Sharon had completely forgotten about the cockroaches and her grandfather. She frowned in bewilderment. What had Skyfighter done for kite supplies?

"We had cedar sap, from the trees — it was very sticky, like syrup. So I used that for my glue. And paper? There was heavy brown wrapping paper. I soaked it in warm water and scraped it to make it lighter. Then I started working on my kites. But I had to work fast. The boss, he turned all the lights out at nine o'clock!"

Sharon grinned because her mom did the same thing on week-nights. It was a real bother if Sharon was in the middle of a good TV show or a good book.

"Down by the ocean, there was always wind. Strong winds with the bite of salt in them to wake you up," continued Skyfighter. "The beach was rocky and it was hard to run there. But once the kite was up, I was a different man. My bones stopped aching, my muscles loosened. I thought I was a seagull, flying free, lighter than air … And somewhere over the horizon I could see my wife's beautiful face, waiting for me."

Skyfighter paused and the faraway look in his eyes vanished. Then he slammed his hand down onto the table with a bang. "They said I was crazy! Told me to stop acting like a child. Told me to act my age! Well, I'm still alive today. You know why? Because I was acting like a twelve-year-old when I was thirty!"

Skyfighter chuckled loudly. "But I didn't mind them. I told them, if you want to fly a kite, just ask. I wanted to share my kites with them! You can't work and sleep your whole life away without finding something to make you smile. I should have told them that the secret of life over death was in the winds. Then they would have lined up to fly my kites!"

Sharon nodded her head enthusiastically in agreement. If she had been there, she would have pushed her way to be first in line. She was sure that Skyfighter was the one to help her teach Samson a lesson about laughing at her. "Dai-bahk," she asked, "Will you help me build a kite like yours?"

Skyfighter let out a long slow breath and shook his head. He held out his hands, and Sharon saw that his fingers were stiff, with swollen knuckles and dry, wrinkled skin. He tried to bend them, and

23

Sharon saw that he could not. "It's too late now, my bones are too stiff. From working out in the cold. Now I can't cut paper or hold the bamboo." He sighed. "And my eyes are bad too."

They sat in silence for a while, listening to the busy street noises from below. Sharon felt sad. She was sorry for Skyfighter, who looked tiny, old, and tired now. Yeh-yeh finished reading the newspaper and put it down softly. He cleared his throat to indicate that it was time for them to go.

Skyfighter looked up from his hands and said, "You don't need a fancy kite for flying, Sharon. In Vancouver, sometimes the wind isn't strong enough. The mountains and islands stop the strong ocean winds from hitting Vancouver directly, you see."

Skyfighter walked over to his table and pulled open a drawer. He took out a small roll of cloth, with a coil of thin wire wrapped around it. "Here, Sharon, try this one," he said. "Goodbye."

Sharon followed Yeh-yeh to the door, and then suddenly whirled around and ran to Skyfighter. She hugged him quickly before joining her grandfather. When they reached the street, Sharon said thank you and goodbye to Yeh-yeh, and hugged him tightly too.

Then she headed up Pender Street, skipping gaily along. She turned the bundled kite over and over like a ball in her hands. Skyfighter had made her feel happy and sad about Yeh-yeh and Chinatown. For the first time in her life, Sharon felt that being Chinese was really okay. If she were not Chinese, she reasoned, she would never have met Skyfighter and heard his story. And she would never have received a special kite from the expert.

Now she wondered why it had taken such a long time for her to discover this feeling. She felt bad for having thought so little of Yeh-yeh. As usual, Pender Street was crowded with Chinese shoppers, who were weighed down with plastic bags crammed with fresh vegetables and groceries. Sharon peered into many passing faces, and guessed that every one probably had stories as interesting as Skyfighter's to tell.

Kite-flying day arrived with a burst of sunshine, blue skies, and a few puffs of cloud. Sharon and Chris were the last to jump off the bus. They were amazed that the driver had not kicked the whole class off earlier for being so noisy. Everyone had been sharing jokes and laughing together on the bus. Now they all raced down to the beach as fast as they could go.

Sharon had lent Eddy's square kite to one of Samson's friends on the bus, and Skyfighter's kite was tucked in her pocket. The two friends walked cheerfully toward the water. Chris was whistling a tune to herself just as if there was no tension in the air at all. Then she asked the question that was on both of their minds.

"Sharon, are you sure that piece of cloth will fly?"

"Sure!" Sharon replied brightly. "I have it on the best authority!" Earlier, Sharon had told Chris about her afternoon with Skyfighter, but Chris was still not fully convinced.

"Are you sure the old man's not a bit crazy?" Chris asked, arching her eyebrows sceptically. "I mean, living alone all those years with a bunch of broken kites? Why didn't he go home to his wife?"

"My grandfather said that Skyfighter believed that Canada was home," Sharon answered, "and by the time the laws were changed, his wife had died."

But the same doubts had crossed Sharon's mind. At home, she had unrolled Skyfighter's cloth kite with great care. She had looked it over and had asked herself, "This is a kite?" She had flapped it about, but could not even see what it was supposed to be. At least the thin light cloth seemed to be in good condition.

27

Sharon had wondered if she could really trust Skyfighter. After all, he had not flown a kite in years. What if the kite flopped in front of Samson? It was the thought of Samson and his friends having the final laugh that bothered her the most. But, in the end, it was Skyfighter's kite that she brought to the beach. She could not believe that a man like Skyfighter who had told her so much, could be wrong.

Samson was just ready to launch his butterfly when the girls arrived on the scene. They could feel a light wind on their faces as they watched the boats chugging out toward the open water. Everyone was gathered around Samson, who held his kite up proudly.

"Unloaded your kite, eh?" challenged Samson in a loud triumphant voice when he spotted the girls.

"Nope, I'm sharing it," Sharon replied. "Besides, I've got another kite to try out on you."

"Oh, yeah?" Immediately Samson was suspicious. "Let's see it! Where is it?"

"In my back pocket," Sharon said casually. When she pulled it out, Samson and his friends burst out laughing. "Sharon, you're nuts! That thing won't fly!"

Sharon ignored them, and folded her arms across her chest. "Go ahead, Samson. Go on and fly yours."

The crowd grew quiet as they watched. Samson licked his finger and held it up to test the wind's direction. Then he had one of his friends hold the kite up high, and he backed off from it, letting off the line bit by bit. The butterfly gleamed like a shiny spaceship in the bright sunlight. Then Samson pulled the string taut and shouted. "Take-off!" and started running as fast as he could. The kite jerked into the air, hung there for a moment, and then crashed to the ground.

Samson raced over and picked it up carefully, inspecting it all around for damage. Finally he announced, "It's okay!" Even Sharon felt relieved, because the butterfly reminded her of Skyfighter's hawk kite. Both of them had been very carefully built. Then Samson tried a second run, shouting, "Hold it higher!" at his friend. But again, the butterfly dropped through the light breeze to the grass and bounced over a few times. It looked as if the butterfly needed a motor or a hurricane to get it going. Today's mild winds were not enough.

Samson tried a third time, and a fourth, but the butterfly refused to fly. Samson checked the wind direction again, but it was no use. He kept his eyes down, refusing to look anyone in the face. No one knew what to say to him.

Sharon unrolled Skyfighter's cloth kite and shook it open. Then she started running too, and right away the breeze caught it and flung it into the sky. Soon the kite was sailing high above the beach. It was shaped like a bat, with wings scooped to catch the slightest breath of wind. Skyfighter was right, Sharon thought. What a genius that man was! The kids were impressed as they watched the bat soar higher and higher.

Sharon felt the wind tugging at her kite. Far above, she saw a seagull carving a wide arc in the sky. The sun was full and warm on her face, and a peaceful glow of satisfaction spread through her body. She could feel every tiny movement of the wind through the kite as it skipped and danced high above. Now I know why people dream of flying, she thought. Now she knew how kite-flying had given Skyfighter times of real happiness through all those hard and lonely years.

Chris was throwing a frisbee with the other kids, and one or two of the others were busy launching their own kites. Some were store-bought diamond-shaped kites, others were shaped like birds. Jane had brought her camera and was taking pictures. And Samson was staring up at her bat-kite, mouth wide open and a hand cupped over his forehead to block the sun. His eyes followed every dip and jump of the kite. The butterfly lay on the ground, forgotten.

Sharon thought of shouting, "Okay, Samson Wong, you bigmouth. Let's see you fly your wonderful kite. Big wings will do it every time, right?"

But now she didn't feel like fighting. She had - nothing to prove to Samson anymore. She was happy just watching her kite pull into the clouds. She had never felt so satisfied and excited in her life. And now she knew it was because the kite and its story were finally Chinese things that made real sense to her.

Skyfighter's kite was made in Canada, not brought from China and dumped on her with a note saying, "This is good for you because it is Chinese." No, the kite and its story were a hundred times better than Chinese school and telling fast jokes in Cantonese.

Sharon remembered Skyfighter's gentle voice and good humour. He had been more than willing to share his kites. "Hey, Samson," she called, "want to take over for me? I want to try the frisbee!"

Samson came racing over. As he took the line from her, he said enviously, "That's a good kite you have. Where'd you get it?"

"From an old man — " Sharon started, but she could not finish the sentence. Skyfighter was not just another old man from Chinatown. "I got it from a new friend," she started again. "A good friend. He's been making kites for the last sixty years."

"Wow! Sixty years!" Samson looked impressed. Then he added, "You want to try flying mine?"

Sharon shook her head. "No, it's too heavy, Samson. It's too heavy for this kind of a wind." Silently she thanked Skyfighter again for his advice.

And Samson said, "I think you're right."

Who Set the Fire?

Who Set the Fire?

AT first, Samson thought the clanging would fade away as soon as the fire truck went down Hastings Street. But tonight, the shriek of the sirens rose higher and higher. Then Samson felt the top of his desk vibrate, just as the fire engine roared right by the Chinese Public School. The whole class looked up expectantly and someone whispered, "Fire!" Excited chatters suddenly crowded the air.

But Mrs. Cheung cleared her throat loudly and stared sternly over the class, so work was reluctantly resumed. Samson wished that she would give the class a break and go outside to investigate. It was almost five o'clock and already dark. Inside the long, narrow classroom, the lamps shone warmly over the panelled walls and the scarred wooden desks, carved with the initials of generations of restless students.

In a few moments, the sirens squealed to a stop, and nothing unusual could be heard. Samson sneaked a glance over at Sharon and John, who were carefully tracing Chinese words into their copy books with thick brushstrokes. Samson's two friends were more patient with Chinese school, and never gave Mrs. Cheung the trouble that Samson did. Last week, she had caught Samson cheating during a test, but Samson just shrugged off her threats.

John's heavy eyeglasses seemed to be pulling his whole body forward. Any time now, John might look up and his nose would be tipped with the wet black ink. As for Sharon, her tanned face was relaxed even in concentration, under her shiny and neatly cut hair. She really enjoyed using the long Chinese brush. Samson, however, hated everything about Chinese school.

Just the other night, Samson had endured another fight with his parents about Chinese school. Classes were held every day after English school. It took time away from hockey. It kept him from watching TV. There was added homework, too.

His mother listened to his loud complaints and shook her head. "You're a Chinese, son. Have you forgotten that? How else will you learn the language?" she asked.

Samson's father had been more abrupt. "Lots of kids go. They don't complain. You'll go!" That had ended the argument immediately because Samson had learned never to fight with his father, who could easily be provoked into giving a spanking.

When Samson's family had come to Canada from Hong Kong four years ago, his parents thought that Samson might forget all his Chinese. They had watched him learn English from school and TV like a thirsty cat lapping up milk. Chinese was spoken at home, but they had worried that Samson might never write a letter to relatives in China. So Samson had found himself put in a Chinese language school with other immigrant kids, like John, and even native-borns like Sharon.

Samson was an only child, and his parents wanted him to do well. But Samson's report cards were only average, and he preferred hockey and TV to his school books. His parents had made rules about study time, but they were hard to enforce. Samson's father was a stock man in a Chinatown supermarket and his mother worked in a laundry. Both worked long hours and sometimes even weekends.

Samson wished his parents could speak better English. They read the Chinese newspaper and listened to the Chinese radio station at home. Sometimes Samson wondered why they had moved to Canada if they were going to keep acting so Chinese. All they wanted him to do was to study all day. Samson liked to take it easy; he did not find the lessons difficult any more. And if his parents were going to force him to go to Chinese school, then he wouldn't bother to bring home good marks for them. He would rather daydream his time away.

Finally, after what seemed like the longest half hour, the bell rang. As the kids streamed eagerly into the hallway and into the cool night air, Samson tried to pull John and Sharon along with him. "Come on," he urged. "Let's go find the fire!"

"Forget it," Sharon squelched him. "It was probably just another false alarm." Samson and Sharon would argue at every chance, even if it wasn't serious. It was more like a game between them. Sometimes Samson thought Sharon acted too smart just because she was Canadian-born. But Samson did not really care, and he would tease her just to show her that he wasn't afraid of her kind.

Right now he was wondering. Maybe she was wrong. Maybe this time there really *was* a fire.

Lately, there had been a rash of false alarms at the elementary school and at the community centre. Nobody knew who was pulling the fire alarms, but many people suspected the kids from the public housing projects. One day, Samson had heard his parents talking about it. His father had worried about what would happen if there was a real fire and the fire trucks did not come.

"There's not much the school can do, is there?" his mother had asked, sounding resigned. She did not speak much English, so she was afraid of many things, one of them being the children from the housing projects, and especially the white ones. The boys were about the same age as Samson, but appeared totally uncontrollable. She had seen them outside the corner store, smoking cigarettes, talking loudly, and pushing each other around. It was even rumoured that they drank liquor secretly and were involved in petty crimes.

"It's the fault of their parents," Samson's father had concluded. "There's no family discipline at home, that's the problem." He looked straight at Samson. "You stay away from them, you hear? I don't want you going into the housing projects."

Samson had nodded. There were Chinese and East Indian families living in the projects too, but his father did not see them as the problem. Samson knew there were troublemakers in those families too.

The noisy crowd of parents and children milling around the door of the Chinese Public School was dispersing quickly. Just four blocks up on Pender Street, the lights of the Raymur housing project highrises glimmered softly. In the other direction, the coloured neon signs of Chinatown's stores and restaurants glittered and twinkled like Christmas decorations.

The three teammates turned away from the lights of Chinatown and headed up Pender Street. Samson itched to dart ahead to see if the fire engines were still around, but Sharon and John were talking about hockey. Samson wanted to hear what they had to say since he was team captain of the Dragons.

Sharon was complaining to John about their archrivals, the Richmond Ravens. The play-offs for the inter-school tournament started next week, and the Ravens were first on the Dragons' list. The Dragons would also play their last league game against the Ravens, whom none of the Dragons liked. "They won last time around only because they played dirty." Sharon was saying. "Remember how that big guy with the kinky hair body-checked Samson? Almost knocked him out cold!"

"He did not!" protested Samson. "I was just —" But before he finished his sentence, something else caught his eye. "Look, the fire!" And the three raced over to the adventure playground next to the community centre.

But there wasn't any fire burning anywhere. In fact, the fire engines were already gone. There were only two police cars stationed there, with their rooftop lights flashing. A crowd of curious onlookers had gathered. As Samson and his friends ran up, the sharp smell of burnt plastic burst into their noses.

"What happened? What happened?" Samson shouted to no one in particular. He tried to break through the circle of backs surrounding the policemen. They were asking questions and taking notes. Samson tried to listen, but couldn't hear what was being discussed. He searched for a familiar face, but it was too dark to see.

Then he saw Sharon and John in the pool of light in front of the community centre door talking to Quang. Quang was also new in their class, one of the many refugee boat people who had settled recently in Strathcona. Samson had asked him about the escape from Vietnam, but Quang had not wanted to talk about it. Samson didn't know whether to feel sorry for him or not.

When Samson got to the doorway, Quang was already gone. "What'd he say?" puffed Samson. "What happened?"

"Nothing much." Sharon shrugged. "Quang said he didn't see anything."

Blast you, Samson thought furiously. As usual, Sharon was pretending to be cool and casual about everything. He turned to John.

"He said that when he got here, someone from the community centre had already put out the fire," John reported.

"Fire? What fire?" Samson pressed impatiently for more information.

"Someone set a garbage can on fire and one of the playground units got burnt."

"What?" Samson's eyes flew wide open. "Who did it?"

"They don't know," answered Sharon as she looked over the circle of people around the police. "That's why the police are asking questions. Maybe someone saw something."

"I don't know who did it, but I bet I know where they came from!" Samson's mind leapt to a conclusion — to him, it seemed obvious.

"How would you know?" demanded Sharon.

"Come on, Sharon, don't play dumb. Everyone knows where trouble comes from!" Samson knew that Sharon suspected the same people, but just didn't want to agree with him.

"Yeah, I know, I know," Sharon replied. "Blame it all on the housing projects."

"Well, it's true, isn't it?" Samson was determined to push his point home. For once, it seemed as if Sharon had taken the losing side of the argument. "The kids from the housing projects think they're so tough! Remember when they crashed the party at — "

"They're not all like that!" interrupted John. "Look at Chris! She lives in MacLean Park, and she's okay."

"Yeah, she even scores more goals than you, Samson," Sharon put in.

"Only because I set her up!" retorted Samson.

"No way! You never pass the puck!"

"I do so! You're the puck hog yourself!"

Then John let out a loud yelp. "Oh, no! It's six-thirty. I'm late for dinner!"

In the excitement, the kids had forgotten all about the time. They raced off in separate directions. To be an hour late meant trouble for sure. Dinner would be waiting and their parents would be impatient. And worried. That was something the kids couldn't understand. What was there to be worried about? This was home territory!

Next day, the grade five class was noisier than usual. It seemed as if the heat of the fire had not yet died down. The adventure playground had been roped off so that no one could get close to it. Before classes, Samson, Sharon, and John joined the crowd of students watching the school engineer inspect the damage. When the bell rang, Sharon looked around for Chris, but could not see her. She didn't show up for school at all.

Ms. Davies, their teacher, was short-tempered and impatient all morning. She had come into class late, with a worried look on her face. Samson liked Ms. Davies. For one thing, she was the sponsor of their hockey team. And she was always interested in hearing what her students had to say. She was not like some other teachers who only pretended to listen to the kids.

Ms. Davies had made the classroom feel warm and comfortable. Plants covered the windowsill and an aquarium with tropical fish sat in another corner. The walls were always covered with drawings and paintings from different school projects.

Today, Ms. Davies did not say a word about the fire, but sharply told the class to quiet down several times. Usually, she just asked the class if they did not think they were getting too noisy. When the recess bell rang, she seemed relieved. Then she asked Sharon to stay behind.

Samson and John traded puzzled looks before racing outside to the adventure playground. Samson was eager to see if anything new had developed. But everything was still roped off, so the boys turned away with disappointed shrugs.

When the boys got back to class, everyone else had already returned, and Ms. Davies was waiting to start the reading exercises. Sharon had her eyes fixed on her hands, which were stiffly clenched on the desk-top before her. Her downcast face suggested that she had been punished. Samson was mystified. What could have happened? Sharon was such a good student that it was hard to imagine her getting into trouble.

When it was Sharon's turn to read, she read in a dull monotone, without putting any life or expression into the words. "Uh-oh," noted Samson, "she's in trouble for sure." He saw that even John had turned to stare at her. Sharon was a good reader and usually performed her lines in a loud and lively voice. Samson figured anyone born in Canada had better be able to read well.

At lunch, Sharon was nowhere to be seen in the noisy, steamy cafeteria. Normally, she sat at a table full of girls. At another table, Samson and the other guys gulped their lunches down as fast as they could, to get away and play. Samson wanted to find Sharon and bug her, but since she was gone, he dashed off to the playing field.

The afternoon went by in a blur — there was library time and then music class. Samson kept thinking about hockey. They played their last league game today and the tournament started next week. The winning team would bring a silver trophy back to display at their school. Last year's winners had even had their picture in the newspaper! Samson hoped that he would be able to show a similar picture, with himself in it, to his parents. Then he remembered that Chris had not shown up for classes today.

"That means I can play centre!" he thought. Whenever Chris ran off with her friends from the housing project, Samson moved over from wing position. The only reason Chris could play better hockey than he could, Samson told himself, was that housing-project life had made her tough.

When Samson arrived in the hockey courtyard, Sharon, John, Cam, Ray, and Man-Chok were waiting there. Samson saw right away that something was wrong by the way they were standing.

"Hey, Samson, bad news!" called out Cam.

"What happened?"

Sharon's face was long and miserable. "Ms. Davies said that Chris has been suspended," she said slowly. "Someone saw her running away from yesterday's fire and reported her."

Samson's mouth dropped open in surprise. For a few seconds he did not know what to say. This was serious! A fire involved policemen, firemen, fire engines, and lots of money!

"I don't believe it," John was saying. "It doesn't sound like her."

"Yeah, I never thought Christine would get into this kind of trouble," agreed Man-Chok, who also lived in MacLean Park.

"Have the police arrested her?" Samson asked.

"No, you dummy! They don't arrest kids!" snapped Sharon. "They're not sure what they want to do. But Ms. Davies said that if we knew anything about Chris and the fire, we should tell her right away."

Samson shook his head. He did not know much about Chris. She lived with her mother because her parents were separated. Her father worked on and off at a mill, but came occasionally to watch the Dragons play hockey. He seemed like a friendly man, who smiled and said hi to all the kids.

Sharon was Chris's good friend, but only when the housing-project kids were not around. Samson doubted if even Sharon knew what Chris did when she hung around with them. But when Chris played hockey, she forgot all about them. And when she joined one of their projects at school, she worked hard.

"I don't believe Chris did it," repeated Ray.

"How do you know?" asked Samson suspiciously. "She's always hanging around with the kids from MacLean Park!"

"Not always!" retorted Sharon. "Just sometimes."

Samson knew that Sharon would defend her friend. "Yeah, but they're the ones who're always getting into trouble," Samson reminded her. "Remember that time when the janitor caught them letting the air out of Mr. Morrison's car tires?" Mr. Morrison was the principal, and a bunch of the MacLean Park kids were trying to get even with him for a detention he had slapped on them.

"Yeah, but Chris wasn't with them that time, was she?"

Samson had to admit that she had not been.

"How long will Chris be suspended?" asked Cam.

Sharon shrugged. "Ms. Davies didn't say. She's going to see Chris tomorrow at home."

"She's going to waste her time," Samson said deliberately.

"Oh, shut up!" exploded Sharon. "You don't know anything! And I don't want to play hockey with a bunch of jerks like you!" She was so angry that she ran off. A second later, the van pulled up, and the Richmond Ravens jumped out for the game.

"What a fine time for her to run off," Samson muttered angrily to himself as he hurried to set things up. There were just enough players to make a team for the Dragons. Samson felt shaky because two key players were absent, but he did not let it show. He wondered if the team could manage.

An hour later, Samson received the grim answer to his question. No, the Dragons could not manage. The game was a disaster, with the Dragons losing by four points. No one had been in the right place for a pass. They had not been able to break up the Ravens' plays. The Dragons needed at least one more person who could pass and shoot as accurately as Sharon.

The Dragons picked up their pads and sticks noisily without anyone saying a word.

"That was the worst game we've ever played," grumbled Man-Chok.

"I hate losing to the Ravens," added Ray. "They play dirty."

Then John asked the question that everyone was worried about. "What are we going to do for the play-offs? Without Sharon and Chris, we don't have a chance."

"We can do without them," Samson declared loudly. "C'mon, we're all guys. We can do it. We'll show those two."

But the others shook their heads. "Maybe you should go talk to Sharon," suggested Ray. "Say you're sorry or something."

"No way!" replied Samson. "If she doesn't want to play, that's her problem. We just have to play harder ourselves, that's all."

Ray shrugged because he knew how difficult it was to change Samson's mind. As the kids headed off in different directions, Samson could hear murmurs of discontent. Samson picked up his equipment alone and trudged off towards the Chinese school. It was true, he realized, that he had provoked Sharon to leave. Now everybody was blaming him. Those guys, Samson thought bitterly, they've all had it too easy. They're not like me.

Samson felt so low that he decided to skip Chinese school again. He dropped his stick and pads onto the ground and hopped onto the broad stone slab by the stairs of Strathcona School's main building. He stretched his legs out and looked across the street to the Chinese school. It seemed certain that the Dragons would lose at the play-offs. But it's not my fault if those guys don't want to try harder, Samson reasoned to himself. And it's not my fault that Chris got suspended.

Whenever Samson felt sorry for himself, he would reach back into the first few years of life in Canada and remember for a while. Then he would get his sense of direction back. After their arrival in Vancouver, his mother had started work immediately at the laundry, but his father had not been able to find work. Samson recalled how he had not wanted to go home at times.

For the first time in his life, Samson had been more afraid for his father than afraid of him. For days, his father said little at dinner and ate even less. He stopped exercising and lost weight. His mother was worried too, but she knew that her husband had to work things out for himself.

Samson's mother had tried not to let Samson feel her own fears and worries about the future. At the dinner table, she always asked what his class was doing at school. Samson was careful never to complain because the last thing his parents needed was more bad news. One day, he brought home a test paper on which he had scored one hundred percent. His mother nodded approvingly and went on eating, but Samson's father seized the sheet of paper and studied it for a long time.

When he looked up, he said, "That's how to go, son. Study hard and watch out for yourself. No one else will help you if you don't help yourself."

This was the first time in weeks that Samson's father had spoken, so Samson remembered every word very clearly. He was thankful that he had not complained, or his father would have thought he was a weakling. And, to be sure, school was a problem.

Even though Samson had been placed in a special language class for new immigrants, there were many times when he did not understand what the teacher was saying. He was also afraid to stick his hand up and say that he didn't understand. He just nodded and tried to listen harder. The other kids in the class spoke Chinese at recess and at lunch, but Samson avoided them.

Their class had played baseball one day, and they had lost so badly that Samson resolved that he never wanted to be a loser. He went home after school every day and watched TV. He tried to study, but it felt hopeless. Then, one day, everything fell into place. It was like waking up after a bad dream. Now all the teacher's sentences made sense to him and English words began to come out of his mouth without his having to think about it.

From that day, Samson had never looked back. He was not going to be a shy, quiet, "New Canadian" student. He was going to try everything. That was one reason for playing hockey.

Samson's thoughts were suddenly interrupted by a voice. "Samson, are you okay?" It was John, speaking in Chinese. "Sorry we lost the game."

"Nothing to be sorry about," answered Samson curtly. "It's that stupid Sharon Fong's fault. Shouldn't you be in class?"

"I told Mrs. Cheung I had a stomach-ache. Sharon wasn't in class either." John paused for a second, and asked in a serious voice, "Do you really think Chris set the fire?"

"How would I know? She's been suspended, hasn't she?" John made no comment here, so Samson continued, "And if she didn't do it, why doesn't she say so?"

"Maybe she's afraid to say who really did it," suggested John.

"Ah, who cares?" Samson threw his hands up in despair. "What can I do, anyway?" He didn't want to hear anything further.

Then John said something really strange. "Sometimes, you and that Chris are the same. Everything is a big test. You've always got to have things your way."

"You're nuts!" replied Samson. "Chris is like me? You've got to be kidding. She's lazy, she hangs around with that gang, and she probably even smokes!"

"So why does she play hockey with us?"

Samson thought that one over for a second, and then for a few more seconds. "I don't know!" he finally growled. "I don't care!"

"Okay, okay," soothed John. "Don't get upset, okay? See you later."

Samson watched John disappear across the street. Useless person, that John, Samson said to himself. Makes trouble wherever he goes. Now what?

Samson knew that he did not want to lose the next game. He knew that he needed at least Sharon back in the team to win. And the only way to get her back was to apologise. No way he was going to do that.

Samson realized that if they lost the next game, it would be the end. No photo in the newspaper. No good news for his parents. The entire year's practices would have been wasted, and the team would blame him. It was his fault for not saying he was sorry. But what could he do now?

Then he knew. He would prove Sharon right or prove her wrong. Right now, no one knew if Chris was guilty or not. Well, he would go and find out, straight from the person who knew — Chris herself. If Sharon was right, that was one thing, but if he was right, then he could get the team together. All he had to do was to go ask. Why hadn't he thought of this earlier, he wondered. Samson jumped off the stairs and headed over to MacLean Park.

The MacLean Park project was made up of low-rise apartments spread over four city blocks. Near the centre of the complex was a high-rise apartment tower for senior citizens. There was concrete everywhere, but most apartments had small green lawns in front of them. Some tenants had planted beds of flowers and rows of vegetables in the small plots.

Samson slowed down when he got close to Chris's apartment. He began to feel nervous again, but he said to himself, I'm not afraid. If I can't do this, then I'm useless. I've got to do this!

Samson took a deep breath and drew himself up to his full height to knock on the door. There was a rattle, and the door opened just a crack. One eye peered out at him from behind the chain.

"Mrs. Thomas?" Samson spoke hesitantly. "Hi, my name is Samson Wong, and I'm the captain of the hockey team that Chris plays on. Can I see her?"

"What for?" asked a weary voice.

"Just … just to see how she is," lied Samson. "Some of her friends are getting worried." Samson heard the chain clatter, and the door swung open. Christine's mother stood back to let him in, and then she limped over to the sofa.

"Come in," she said. "I've got to sit down myself. I just got home from work." Mrs. Thomas was wearing a dark- coloured waitress's smock with her name tag pinned to it. Samson looked curiously around the room, since this was his first visit to a white family's home. The soft old sofa, rug, clock, and plants were not too different from those at home. The only difference was that the room was really tiny. And through the wall Samson could hear the TV from the apartment next door.

"Chris is in her room," explained Mrs. Thomas. "I don't know what she's doing." She leaned back and closed her eyes.

Samson wondered if Mrs. Thomas knew anything about the fire, but he wasn't sure how to approach the subject. Finally he asked cautiously, "Do … do you think she's in trouble? I mean, do you think she set the fire?"

Mrs. Thomas answered slowly, "I want to say no, she didn't. But honestly, Samson, I don't know. I don't spend enough time with her these days. I work, and then I'm all tired out."

His mother was like that too, Samson thought. When she came home from the laundry, she would sit for a few minutes before starting to cook supper. It was always hard to talk to her at this time. After the dishes were washed, she would sip her tea slowly to relax, but there was always more housework to be done. At least I don't make trouble for my mother, Samson told himself.

"Chris!" Mrs. Thomas had raised her voice and was calling, "Chris, your friend is here!"

Nothing happened. Mrs. Thomas was about to get up, but Samson stopped her. "Don't get up," he said. "Which room is it?"

Mrs. Thomas waved gratefully towards a door. "Thanks, Samson," she said. "You don't know how tired I am. I'm glad you came, I really am." And a weak smile darted across her face.

"Chris?" Samson knocked softly on the door. "Chris, are you there?" There was no answer, and

Samson knocked again, loudly. Then he waited. "Chris?" he called.

"Go away!" came the reply.

"Chris, it's me, Samson!" He paused, and then pushed the door open and peeked in. Chris was lying on her bed, face down.

Samson edged into the room on tiptoe. He stopped before getting too close and asked, "Chris, are you okay?"

There was no answer, and Samson could feel himself getting a bit angry. He had come all this way to talk, and now she would not even look at him. Sure, he and Chris had never been good friends, but things were different right now. She was in trouble and he was trying to help.

"Hey, Chris," he ventured. "Want some gum?" He pulled out a package and held it out as he went over to the bed. "It's Super Bubble!"

When there was no response again, Samson stuffed a few pieces into his own mouth. His eyes roamed around the room. Chris had pinned pictures of TV stars and hockey players to her walls. There was an old box by her bed with a clock and a lamp on it. Comic books and magazines spilled out from under her bed just like Samson's books did at home.

Chris had not moved one bit. Samson wondered if she thought Ms. Davies had sent him over to spy on her. He started to blow bubbles with his gum, now that it was soft and stretchy.

"We lost to the Ravens today," he started again. "It was a real wipe-out!" Then he added, "Sharon didn't play either."

When there was still no answer from Chris, Samson decided that there was nothing else to do but to ask about the fire. "Everyone is wondering about you," he said. "Not everyone thinks that you set the fire."

"Oh, yeah?" came a muffled retort. "Who?"

"Sharon, for one," Samson answered quickly. "And John, and Ray. Cam and Man-Chok too. We were all just talking about it."

Chris thought for a second before she turned her head. "I'll bet you were. The whole hockey team, right? Hah! You guys are more worried about the play-offs!"

Bang! The bubble exploded like a gunshot. And suddenly Samson's face was covered with sticky pink chewing gum. There was even some in his eye, blinding him momentarily.

Chris burst out laughing with a yelp of delight. Her hoots of laughter surrounded Samson as he furiously tried to clean himself. "It's not funny," he sputtered.

"Yes, it is," Chris insisted.

When her laughter died down, Samson asked again, "What happened that night? Tell me, Chris." When she continued to hesitate, he pressed, "Why don't you trust me?"

"It's just that all of you Chinese are so goody-goody!" Chris exclaimed. "You never get into trouble. It's like you're on the teacher's side all the time."

"But we get into trouble too," argued Samson. "Remember the chalk fight last week?"

That brought a smile to Chris's face. "Yeah, that was fun!" she agreed. "You got sent to Mr. Morrison's office." And they both grinned at the memory of the flurry of chalk bits hurtling through the air like a snowstorm. Then Chris looked at Samson closely and said, "Okay, but you better not tell anyone."

"Chris, you can trust me," exclaimed Samson.

"I didn't set the fire," she said. "David Mitchell did."

David Mitchell? Samson was not surprised at all. David lived in MacLean Park too and was also in their class. He was a small skinny fellow with nervous eyes that darted about like those of a hungry bird looking for food. David skipped a lot of classes, and even when he was present, he was quiet and sullen. Maybe he was sick a lot.

"I was coming out of the centre," continued Chris, "when I saw a flicker of light in the playground. Then I saw another flash, real quick, so I ran over to check it out. When I got there, David was there, fooling around. He had this old lighter that he was trying to work, but it was too windy. There must have been a bit of gasoline or something in the garbage can. The next thing I knew, there was a swoosh, and flames were shooting everywhere. We took off as fast as we could."

"But why did you run?" Samson asked. "You didn't do anything."

Chris shrugged. "Who'd have believed me?"

"Aren't you going to tell Ms. Davies the truth?" When Chris shook her head, Samson was startled. "You can't cover up for a criminal!" he insisted. "Setting fires is serious."

"David's a kid," Chris replied. "I'm not finking on one of us."

"But if David did it, he should take the blame, not you," argued Samson.

"Listen, Samson," Chris said slowly, as if to stop the argument. "I'll never tattle on another kid.

And that's that. And if you tell, I'll break your neck."

Samson sighed and stared gloomily at the floor. There did not seem to be an easy answer anywhere. "Wait a minute," he said suddenly. "What if we get David to tattle, to tell on himself? Maybe he can say that it was an accident."

"He'd never do it," Chris said doubtfully.

"Can you think of anything else?" pushed Samson. "You want to play in the play-offs, don't you?"

Chris looked down and rubbed her hands together thoughtfully. Samson could tell that she wanted to play. And why not? Chris was a very good player who really enjoyed the game when she played. In fact, there wasn't any game or sport that Samson could think of that Chris did not do well in.

Finally Chris agreed to go and see David. She grabbed her jacket as they went out. They hurried over to another row of apartments. Samson had his fingers crossed in hopes that things would work out. They turned a corner and practically knocked down a familiar figure. It was Sharon.

"Watch where you're going!" she sputtered at Samson. "And where *are* you going?"

"Oh, to talk to someone," answered Chris.

"Who?"

"Someone," replied Chris evasively. "Someone who's in trouble."

"So you didn't do it, right?" cried Sharon. "I knew it!" She turned triumphantly to Samson. "See, I told you she didn't do it."

Samson turned a bit red and felt like punching Sharon. "Well," he said, "I didn't think so either. That's why I came to see her."

"Oh, sure," sniffed Sharon. "You're just worried about the play-offs. So who set the fire?"

"David Mitchell," blurted out Samson. Chris jabbed him sharply in the ribs.

"You dummy!" she cried. "You promised not to tell."

"Yeah, but you would've told Sharon anyway," replied Samson defensively. He felt his face grow red again because he didn't like to have people think that he had a big mouth.

Sharon wasn't interested in listening to Samson and Chris argue, and asked them what they were planning to do now.

Samson explained the plan, and Sharon decided to go with them. When they approached the Mitchells' unit, they heard a man's loud angry voice. Then there were some thumps and a child's screams of pain. The three friends stopped in front of David's door. The fighting and crying came clearly from David's home. Samson looked at Chris with alarm. "What's going on?" he asked.

Then the door burst open and David came flying through like a spinning football. Samson was not sure if David had been hurled out or if he had jumped out himself. David picked himself up, moaning and sobbing. Samson saw a dark bruise forming on David's cheek. When David saw his visitors, he turned and dashed away.

Chris shook her head. "That's another reason you can't tell on David. It would just be another excuse for his father to beat him."

Samson was still shaking from the incident. "Does he do that a lot?" he asked.

"Only when he's drunk," answered Chris grimly. "You've never seen anything like that before, have you?"

Samson said no.

"Well, it doesn't go on all the time here," Chris said. "David's dad has really got problems."

When Samson arrived home, he felt like a wire spring that was being pushed in from both ends. He plopped himself in front of the TV to wait for his father and dinner. He still hadn't figured out how to get Chris back onto the team. And the afternoon in MacLean Park had been exhausting.

How could a father treat his own son so badly? Samson's father spanked him, but he never threw him around or kicked him out of the house. Samson shivered to think what it would be like to live with parents that you were scared of.

Then he heard his father slam the door as he came in. Samson knew instantly that something was wrong because his father never slammed the door. Then he heard his father call him to the kitchen. Samson's hands and feet suddenly felt icy cold.

His father had a ferocious scowl on his dark face. The bamboo-handled duster that he used for spanking lay in readiness on the table. Samson's mother was washing vegetables for dinner at the sink. Samson trembled before his father's anger and waited for the bad news. He suspected his father had found out that he'd skipped out of Chinese school that afternoon.

Samson's father struggled to keep his temper under control. He clenched his hands together and massaged them deeply. "Someone told me you didn't go to Chinese school today," he started. "Where did you go?"

"Nowhere," stammered Samson, trying to look innocent.

"Liar. You went into the housing project, into someone's home. And you came out with a girl. Didn't you?"

Samson nodded weakly and wondered who his father's source of information was.

"Who told you to go in?" his father demanded.

Samson remained silent.

"This time, what game were you playing?"

"I … I wasn't playing," started Samson. His father picked up the duster and Samson's heart leapt into his mouth. "I didn't go there to play," he pleaded with his father. "I had to go find out who had set the fire."

"What?!" His father's eyes practically jumped out of their sockets in surprise. "What does the fire have to do with you?"

Slowly, Samson related the story of Chris's suspension, his visit to MacLean Park, and David's beating. His mother stopped her cooking to listen. Samson's mouth was dry by the time he was finished. He looked fearfully at his father, who seemed even more tired now as he rubbed his eyes.

"You stupid boy," he finally said. "I want you to go to Chinese school. I won't use the duster on you today, but if you skip classes again, I will beat you until you're soft. Do you understand?"

Samson sagged in relief when his father left the kitchen to go to wash up. It was a good thing that his father's temper could subside as fast as it erupted. There was still one question on Samson's mind. "Ma," he asked, "who told him about me skipping school?"

"What does it matter?" she replied, busily chopping meat. "Do you want to get even with them? Is that it?"

"No, no," murmured Samson thoughtfully. He had not expected his parents to reveal the name of their friend. Then he looked up with a wide grin on his face. He had just discovered the solution to his problem! All he had to do was tell the truth about the fire to Mr. Morrison, but leave out David's name!

He could explain everything, how it was almost an accident, and how Chris had nothing to do with it. And he could even tell why he could not give David's name. But what if Mr. Morrison refused to believe him? After all, he had been in the principal's office just last week for the chalk fight. Then Samson smiled. He'd thought of a way to solve that problem, too.

On Monday, there was a great cheer in the courtyard when Chris appeared, hockey stick over her shoulder and a smile across her face. Samson could feel that they were going to play a good game. Everyone was so glad to see Chris back again that it did not seem to matter if they won or lost the game.

"Thanks, guys," Chris was saying, "I don't know what you did, but everything's fine now!"

Samson had never been so nervous in his life when he and the entire hockey team had walked into Mr. Morrison's office the Friday before. Samson had started talking very slowly, telling him everything he had heard and seen on his visit to MacLean Park. Mr. Morrison looked at him steadily throughout, and made a few notes.

Samson also explained why the entire team had come. "I thought you might think that I was lying. So, if you don't believe me, then you can ask Sharon, or John, or Man-Chok here." At that point, everyone chimed in loudly to support Samson's story.

Mr. Morrison finally calmed them down and said that he believed Samson's story. Then he asked for David's name, but Samson explained about the beating that would follow.

Mr. Morrison sat back for a few moments. Then he said, "I think I know whom you're referring to. The family has serious problems, and a social

worker is trying to help. Maybe I shouldn't inter-
fere now."

"What about Chris, sir?" Sharon reminded
him.

"Well, she should have come to me earlier. The
trouble with you kids is that you think you can
solve everything by yourselves." He smiled.
"Well, sometimes even grown-ups can help. Chris
will be back at school on Monday."

And so it was. Now Samson noticed a lone
figure watching them from behind the fence. It
was someone who had never come to watch them
play. It was David Mitchell. And when Samson
waved at him, David waved back.

Never Be Afraid!

Never Be Afraid!

JOHN Chin crept along the tiled roof, as swift and silent as a panther. His eyes pierced through the deep black night and scanned the guards pacing beneath the lanterns. The years of martial arts training allowed him to detect the slightest whisper of danger. He gauged the distances and planned his attack. He would leap down and then somersault backwards into the centre.

"Fools," he thought as he unsheathed his sword, "they've left their spears leaning against the wall. They're as good as dead … Now!"

"Hey, John! Come on!"

John jolted back to the present with a start. "The line's moving," said Sharon as she nudged him along. "Daydreaming, huh?"

"Thinking of girls, John?" teased Samson. "Or were you fighting in the movies again?"

John's ears reddened in embarrassment. He was always getting caught by someone when he was deep into one of his fantasies. Sometimes John

72

felt that he couldn't do anything properly. For one thing, he spoke English with an accent. When he tried to say something, he would often wind up using the wrong words. During reading exercises, he tried to read softly so that people would not hear him, but Ms. Davies would always remind him to raise his voice.

And yesterday in hockey, he had flubbed it again. He had let in an easy goal when the other team's centre had broken through and had come rushing straight at him. John had tensed up so quickly that he could not move, and that goal had cost the Dragons the game. Samson had said that it was the defence's fault, but John blamed himself.

John knew that he had not been scared, but his body insisted on misbehaving. More than anything, John wanted to have a shut-out game. Maybe then the Dragons would come up and clap him on the shoulder and shout, "Good game, John!" in the same way that they congratulated one another when someone scored.

John glanced behind and saw that the line-up still stretched down the block in front of the theatre and around the corner. John, Samson, and Sharon had been waiting for an hour, and everyone was feeling restless and impatient. The shoppers and passers-by had stared in amazement at the length of the line-up. John felt himself getting excited about finally seeing this film.

Everyone else in his class had already seen the latest sequel to *Star Wars*, and Samson and Sharon were here for their second and third times. The three of them had been talking one day after hockey, and Sharon had been flabbergasted when she discovered that John had not seen it yet.

"I'm going on Saturday with my brother," she offered. "You can come if you want. It's a great movie!"

John was a bit embarrassed by the offer, and looked at Samson. "Want to go?" he asked.

"Sure!" replied Samson.

Then, as it turned out, Eddy had to cram for an exam and couldn't go, but the kids went anyway.

It was a real treat for John to go to a movie. On Saturdays, John usually helped in the grocery store that his family tended for John's uncle. When the Chins had lived briefly in Hong Kong, they had gone to a few movie theatres there. But since arriving in Canada eighteen months ago, they had had to be very careful about how they spent their money.

In Vancouver, John had only been to the movie theatres close by Chinatown, which showed films from Hong Kong and Taiwan. As for Samson, it sounded as if he had visited every single movie house in town. He was in the middle of telling Sharon all about the deluxe sound system inside this theatre. John often felt jealous of Samson, who had been born in Hong Kong. John, who had spent the first several years of his life in a farming village in China, always felt that he was slower than the Hong Kong kids, who were such "city folks." Samson had learned English very quickly, and he spoke it perfectly, like Sharon.

The line-up began to move quickly now. A murmur of delight snaked down the line through the eager movie-goers, who were mostly children. John grinned at his friends. Suddenly two older boys, dressed in grubby jeans and patched-up jackets, stepped into the line just in front of John. John could hear them chuckling to themselves about not having to wait.

Sharon reached up and tapped the shoulder of one fellow. "Hey," she said. "The line-up starts around the corner."

There was no response. Samson spoke up too. "You guys are supposed to … "

But before he could say another word, one fellow spun around and shoved Sharon into John. The two stumbled back and fell to the ground. John's eyeglasses went flying into the air. The other boy went for Samson, but Samson's left arm shot up instantly. The attacker grunted in surprise when his arm was deflected harmlessly to the side. Samson's right arm darted out and his fingers clasped the bully's throat for a moment. Then Samson dropped back into a "ready" position, with his legs out and arms loose and up close to his chest.

The two intruders stared at each other for a second before running off as fast as they could. There was some scattered applause as the witnesses expressed their approval. As John picked his glasses and himself up, he could feel himself trembling. Everything had happened so quickly. Samson's moves had been so deft and sure that they looked like automatic reflexes.

"Wow!" exclaimed Sharon, as she got up. "Where'd you learn that?"

"I didn't know you knew kung-fu," added John in surprise. "Who taught you?"

Samson seemed embarrassed. "It's nothing," he said. "My father taught me a few moves."

"Is he a *see-fu?*" asked John, referring to the masters who taught the martial arts.

"No," answered Samson. "He was a bank guard in Hong Kong, so he knew some self-defence, that's all."

"You're pretty good," complimented Sharon. "It was like watching a Chinese movie. Hey, we can make our own! We'll make you a star, Samson!" And they all laughed.

"Do you practise a lot?" Sharon continued.

"Nah," replied Samson.

"I guess you don't have to when you're good, eh?" offered John.

Samson looked pleased, but he didn't pursue the subject. "Yeah, it gets kind of boring after a while. It's not my kind of fun anyway."

Then the line moved again and Samson turned away. John was puzzled that Samson did not seem more eager to talk about kung-fu. Usually Samson was so confident about everything he did that people got tired of his bragging. Even Sharon noticed the difference, but she only shrugged when John caught her eye and frowned.

John was relieved that nothing had developed from the incident. The line-up moved along smoothly now. But John was still shaking inside. What would he have done if Samson had not been there? Pushed back? Or would he have backed off, and let the two bullies have their way? Either way, he would have made a fool of himself. Maybe, he thought, as he stuck his money through the wicket, I should learn kung-fu too.

Two days later, John had decided. Yes, he was going to learn kung-fu. The theatre incident was the closest he had ever been to a real fight, and he did not want it ever repeated. It was time to show people that short and skinny kids who wore glasses, like him, were neither weaklings nor cowards. John had checked at the community centre and at the studios in the neighbourhood that offered lessons. Now all he needed was his father's permission.

John's family lived behind the Lucky Star Grocery on Hastings Street, the main road leading to downtown Vancouver one way and out to Burnaby and the suburbs the other way. The store and building were owned by John's uncle, who had helped the Chins immigrate to Canada. The grocery store was open from ten o'clock in the morning until eleven o'clock at night, seven days a week. John and his mother helped out whenever they could in the evenings and on the week-ends.

Mr. Chin kept the tall shelves neatly stocked with canned foods and drinks of all kinds, and a variety of other goods such as soaps, cereals, paper towels, and spices. There was a wide cooler with sliding glass doors, filled with fresh milk, dairy products, and fruit juices. John's favourite job was to restock the candy trays with the chocolate bars and sweets that were bought at the wholesale. But it was like window shopping, because John was not allowed to eat any of the candies.

Behind the storefront were the living quarters. John's parents had one room to themselves, his grandmother shared a room with John's little sister Siuyee, and John had the smallest room to himself. From his bedroom, John could hear the cooler humming through the night. The Chins' TV set sat out in the store, on top of a high shelf. John's father watched it at night in hopes of improving his English.

John's grandmother kept the kitchen spotlessly clean, even as she took care of Siuyee. The kitchen had a big round table, covered with a heavy sheet of clear plastic, around which everything happened. The meals were eaten there, John did his homework at one end, and his mother spread her sewing out over the top.

That evening, the Chins did not sit down to supper until well after seven o'clock. John's grandmother had prepared herb soup, fish with black bean sauce, and stir-fried vegetables to eat with the bowls of steaming rice. John's mother had come home late from her job at the garment factory. John hoped that there would not be many customers coming in, because every time the bell over the front door tinkled, John's father would put his chopsticks down and go out front to serve the customers.

John spoke in the village dialect they used at home. "Ba-ba?" he said, using the Chinese word for "dad."

"What?"

John swallowed nervously. "I want to learn kung-fu."

His father raised an eyebrow. "Where?" he grunted.

"Over on Heatley Street, there's a school there. A Mr. Lim teaches there," John replied. "It's every Saturday morning, from ten until one."

John's mother sat down heavily and sipped the hot soup slowly. She looked tired, and waited to see what her husband would say. Ba-ba always had the final say in all family matters, but her opinion was important too.

"What about your homework?" asked his father between large mouthfuls. He always had to hurry through dinner in order to get back to the store. "When will you get your work done?"

"I can finish it on Friday nights," John promised.

His father thought things over. "John, start eating," urged his mother. "The food will be cold if you don't eat."

John scrambled to fill his mouth, while keeping an anxious eye on his father. Mr. Chin was a tall lean man, who always wore his hair neatly trimmed and combed. He had the largest pair of hands that John had ever seen. The strength in them had been built up from his years of farm work in China before his departure for Hong Kong. John's mother had a broad round face framed by a curly mop of hair, and a soft chubby body to match. She loved to eat all kinds of sweet snacks.

Finally Ba-ba spoke. "Why do you want to learn kung-fu?" he asked. "You looking for trouble? You've been going to too many movies!"

John stammered, "No, I don't want to fight. I … I just want to try it out … to see what it's like."

"Are you sure you can learn?" demanded Ba-ba. "You're such a weakling. You're not strong, do you know that?"

John sagged before his father's remarks, and his eyes pleaded with his mother for help. She was the one who really kept the close eye on John's clothing, schooling, and his everyday needs. John could usually count on her for a sympathetic hearing.

"They're just playing," she spoke thoughtfully. "There's no harm in learning. He'll get stronger. Someday it could be useful."

At that moment, the doorbell tinkled, and John's father rose from the table.

"Ba-ba?" asked John fearfully.

"Remember, you were once a boy too," his mother said to Ba-ba.

"All right, go," he said to John. "Go and try it. But you better not get into any fights, hear? And take care of those eye-glasses of yours. I can't keep buying new ones for you."

John nodded readily, but still he sighed. His glasses had posed a problem ever since he got them two years ago. He had broken his first pair during a soccer game. Then he thought he would keep them in his pocket during sports. But that turned into a disaster when he tripped and fell on them. A third pair of glasses had been lost somewhere.

John's father was angry enough that John even needed glasses. He thought that John's bad eyes came from reading too much, but the doctor said no, reading could not harm them. John's father then concluded that his son was just born on the weak side. As for hockey, it had already claimed John's fourth pair of glasses, so now he played goalie. It was the only position that came with a face mask, and John wore a baseball catcher's mask over his face. He preferred the speed of playing forward or defence, but he knew that if anything should happen to this pair of glasses, he would be in deep trouble. In the meantime, John had learned to live with his glasses.

After the dishes were cleared away and the table wiped clean, John brought his homework out. His grandmother did the dishes, humming old opera tunes to herself as she worked. John's mother had taken Siuyee into her lap to play. John knew that she had a soft spot in her heart for babies. If the Chins hadn't needed the money she earned at the factory, she would happily have stayed home to be a mother.

John opened his textbooks and stared at them for a while. But it was hard to get started. Already he could see himself kicking, punching, and slashing with his bare hands and feet. Or maybe he would use his own secret weapons, the killer coins that he could spray at his enemies like a handful of bullets. "*Ee* yaah!" he screamed, as he fought off a menacing circle of deadly enemies.

John itched to pull out his kung-fu comic books, but if his mother caught him reading those on a school night, she might tear them up. John tried to concentrate on his schoolbooks, but his mind soon flew off to ancient China. Back then, men and women would train from childhood, up in the mist-shrouded mountains. Breathing techniques, swordsmanship, body control, and all the martial arts were practised until they became second nature. The trainees would become the fittest and fastest human beings on the earth.

Many times, John had imagined himself nipping through the air to land gracefully atop the telephone wires high above. The knights of the olden days were in total control of everything. The sneaky or sudden approach of evil was instantly sensed. They would leap over walls like cats and wield their swords like whips. Every fighter had his own style of sword-play, with special techniques and secret moves to dazzle the opponent.

Then there was the art of Chinese boxing, kung-fu fighting with the bare hands and feet. With the proper training, it was possible to kill someone without using any weapon at all. There had been a superstar named Bruce Lee whom the movie crowds in Hong Kong had flocked to see when kung-fu became popular in the West. Some people even had their hair cut like Bruce Lee's. It had been so funny that John laughed aloud at the memory. When his mother looked up in surprise, John buried his head in his books.

"There are many styles of kung-fu," said Mr. Lim as he started the first lesson, "with different names and techniques. Many of them follow the natural movements of animals who have to fight for their daily survival. The forms were developed and refined over many centuries by Buddhist monks in their temples. They used the movements to discipline their minds and bodies as part of their meditation."

John listened impatiently and waited anxiously for the teaching to start. People of various ages and different backgrounds had enrolled in the class. John stole glances at the rack of weapons that stood to the side. There were spears, halberds, pitchforks, and steel-tipped rods, as well as straight and curved swords in their sheaths. One day soon, John thought to himself, I'll be the best fighter around!

Soon the lesson began. At first, there were some warm-up stretches, to loosen the muscles and to develop flexibility. Next, Mr. Lim discussed and demonstrated stance and position, balance and movement, and then basic principles of self-defence. Then he started the class in some grappling moves for close range combat.

Soon Mr. Lim had the class working in pairs. One partner would attack while the other would block. The students tried to apply some of the basic moves that had just been shown to them. John found that he really had to think, because sometimes it was better to raise the left arm instead of the right, or faster to swing in from the outside instead of out from the inside. And at other times, a vertical block was more natural than a horizontal one.

John was paired with Winston Choy. He had seen Winston before, in the adventure playground, usually by himself because he didn't seem to have many friends. Winston didn't appear to recognize John, but started talking almost right away. "This Mr. Lim is supposed to be really good," he told John in a low voice. "He used to be the personal bodyguard to some big shot in the government. He was even an adviser to the kung-fu movies! Did you see that one called *The Boxer's Blood?* Wow!"

Winston went on talking and John would say, "Really?" and, "Oh yeah?" every now and then. But he was trying hard to concentrate on his kung-fu. It was good to work with Winston, who seemed to know what he was doing. Winston was very sure and steady in his movements, and John guessed that he had taken kung-fu lessons before. They fell into a natural rhythm, back and forth, thrusting and blocking, shifting weight and then back again.

After a while, Winston's blows began to thud into John with increasing strength. It hurt, but Winston hardly noticed and John was determined not to let it show.

"Okay, that's enough," called Mr. Lim, who had been moving around the room correcting his students. When he had passed by John and Winston, he had nodded. Now he looked at them again. "You," he said, pointing at Winston. "You look strong. Come over here. I want you to be part of the demonstration."

Winston walked to the front of the room as all the students gathered around. Mr. Lim was waiting with a girl by his side. John recognized her from school too. She was in one of the junior grades. She must have just arrived in the studio, because John had not noticed her earlier.

Mr. Lim introduced her. "This is my daughter Elaine. She is nine years old."

Winston and Elaine stood facing each other with an arm's length in between them. Mr. Lim told them to stand in a "ready" position, and the two youngsters obeyed. Winston grinned confidently at his opponent and out to the audience. Elaine, who was slightly built, looked nervous and anxious. Her slender shoulders quivered noticeably as she put her hands up under her chin and looked at her father.

"All I want Elaine to do is to reach out and tap Winston's chest. And Winston, I want you to stop her. Don't let her touch you. Ready?"

They nodded. John looked intently at them. He wondered if Elaine knew some kung-fu secrets that her father had taught her. John assumed she had to be a good fighter. Some of the best fighters in the movies were women, who fought as long and as hard as men.

Elaine's fist darted at Winston, who reacted right away. But he was a second too slow. Elaine's fist had already touched his shirt when his arm met hers. Winston looked a bit surprised. "Try again," said Mr. Lim.

John saw Winston narrowing his eyes and tensing his arms as he waited for Elaine's next move. Her arm flashed out again, fast but without any strength behind it. Again Winston was late. They tried it twice, and each time Elaine broke through. On the last try, Winston blocked with so much force that Elaine's arm was sent flying backwards.

"That's enough. Thank you, Winston," said Mr. Lim as a relieved-looking Elaine ran off. Then he addressed the class. "Elaine has never learned any kung-fu in her life." There were some surprised murmurs from the students.

"What I wanted to show you is that strength by itself does not count in kung-fu. Winston here is a strong young man, but you need more than strength to fight. Sometimes, using too much strength can even be a disadvantage.

"You have to watch position. You should never stand that close to someone and wait for an attack. At that distance, you have to attack first. Either that or step back. A second thing to beware of is tension. If you tighten up your muscles, you'll slow yourself down. Elaine was faster than Winston because her arm was loose and without power. So, know your strength, relax, and learn to be flexible. That's all for today."

"You were right," a deeply impressed John said to Winston as they stepped outside. "He is a good teacher." Mr. Lim's demonstration of such a simple idea made John want to learn kung-fu more than ever before. Who knew what other secrets Mr. Lim would share with them?

Winston seemed a bit upset over his performance. "I guess so," he agreed reluctantly. "But you still have to be strong. I've never seen weaklings fight and win in the movies, that's for sure!"

In the following weeks, John lived for kung-fu. He practised each and every exercise and movement they learned, whenever he could. On his way to school, his mind would rehearse a set. If he found himself alone in a room, he would get into position and practise moving faster and faster. But he always checked first to see that no one was watching. It would be too embarrassing to have to explain what he was doing. Besides, his friends and family would probably laugh at him.

John was determined to learn kung-fu as thoroughly and as swiftly as possible. Winston seemed just as eager, and the two of them never missed a class. John had never felt himself want anything so badly, and for such good reasons too. He was learning to protect himself, he was strengthening his body, and he was learning a new skill. He felt that he was finally doing something that he really wanted for himself. Sometimes his body ached all over, but John was convinced that it would be worthwhile. "I'll show them," he muttered to himself as he thought of the Dragons. "I can be good at something too!"

One day he would be known and respected. He would walk into a busy Chinatown restaurant with his sword slung across his back, and the waiters would scurry to serve him. After the meal, he would take the coins for the waiters' tip and fling them into the wall with a flick of his wrist, embedding them there like nails.

And if the police should be chasing some robber down the street, John would leap into the air over the heads of passersby and over the tops of cars and trucks to land lightly in front of the astonished criminal. "Slow down," he would say with a slow and knowing smile. "Where do you think you're going?" John would look deceptively slim and small, but his body would be packed with power and ready to block or subdue any move the thief made. And then John's name would be in all the newspapers …

Mr. Lim opened the studio on Sunday for the students to use to practise on their own but John couldn't go. Even if he was excused from helping in the grocery store, there was always hockey practice. He had already missed several practices and a few games. John knew that the one extra player on the team could fill in for him, but Samson, the team captain, was not pleased, and John hoped it would not end in a confrontation. He still wanted all the Dragons, and especially Samson and Sharon, to be his friends.

But in a strange way, John was glad to get away from hockey. Playing goalie always put him in the background of things. If the Dragons won a game, then the ones who had scored were the heroes. The team won more games than it lost, so John felt all right. But not a single Dragon had ever told him that he was doing okay as the goalie. Now that he'd missed a few games, John thought the team might finally realize how badly they needed him.

One Sunday, John found himself with a free afternoon. He knew that he should join the Dragons for a practice but instead, he found himself heading over to Mr. Lim's. He hoped that today he would find the key move to unlock all the secrets of kung-fu. It was the same thought that popped into his mind every time he went to class. When he arrived, Winston was there, rehearsing a shadow-boxing set that they had just learned. These longer sets combined specific arm and leg movements into a dance-like exercise which would become smooth and powerful through practice.

Winston was working hard as he punched and kicked his way through the set. He let out loud grunts as he timed his breathing to match the points of contact against his imaginary foe. John stood behind Winston and started to follow him. But where

Winston was quick and graceful, John was sometimes stiff and a bit uncertain. John could feel himself tensing in frustration, even though his errors were minor ones.

Winston was soon all sweaty, and he went to sit down. John joined him. "Why don't you come more often on Sundays?" asked Winston. "It's good to have the extra practice."

"I usually have hockey practice," explained John.

"Hockey?" snorted Winston. "What a waste of time! Are you on the team that Samson Wong is captain of?"

John nodded in surprise. "You know Samson?"

"No, but his father taught him kung-fu, right? They say he's really good. I'd like to see his stuff one day."

"He is good," asserted John, and went on to describe Samson's brief fight at the theatre. "But you won't see his stuff," he finished. "Samson doesn't like to fight."

Winston shook his head grimly and declared, "He's stupid! Fights like that prove we have to protect ourselves. Man, they're always picking on the Chinese, especially us new immigrants."

John was silent. Winston's last words seemed to echo some of his own feelings. "Sometimes I wish I had never come here," continued Winston. "You call this home? Little kids laughing at my English, people looking down on me all the time. I'll show them!" And with that, he ran to the mirrors to practise some more.

So that was why Winston was so crazy about kung-fu, John thought. Well, John knew that the big change for immigrants came when they stopped feeling like strangers and started feeling like they belonged here. Maybe it was better to do Canadian things like hockey instead of Chinese things like kung-fu, he told himself. It made it easier to adapt and feel at home. At kung-fu, some people spoke Chinese. They might as well be in China. But hockey was nothing if not Canadian. Still, John wondered, did it really matter what you did? He would always look Chinese.

"Come on," called Winston, who had finished. "Let's go get a red bean soda."

They walked up the block towards Chinatown, and Winston started telling John about the latest kung-fu movie he had seen in Chinatown. They had come up to the courtyard where the Dragons were practising before John realized it was too late to walk around. He hoped his teammates wouldn't spot him. But Samson called out as they passed, and ran up to them.

"Listen, John," he announced angrily. "This isn't working. Either you start coming to practice all the time or you quit so we can get ourselves a new goalie."

John was taken aback. He figured Samson must have had a rough day. The rest of the Dragons had gathered behind Samson. "Well, what's it going to be, John?"

John looked from face to face, hoping to find an encouraging smile somewhere. If anyone had said, "We really need you, John," he would have quit kung-fu right then and there. But everyone appeared strained and unhappy, and they avoided his eyes. "Okay," John finally sighed reluctantly. "I quit. I guess you guys really don't need me."

John started to walk away, but he really did not want to leave like this. Suddenly he had a new idea, and he turned back. "Hey, why don't you guys join the kung-fu class? There's a really good teacher."

"Forget it," cried Ray. "A lot of that kung-fu movie stuff is just a bunch of faking around."

John saw Winston's face flinch in response. Sharon voiced her opinion, too. "I'd rather play hockey. I like team sports, they're more fun."

"Yeah, there's more action here. Hockey is Canada's national sport, didn't you know?" Chris announced sarcastically as she raised her stick in a mock salute. And they all laughed when Sharon and Chris snapped to attention to sing *O Canada* in low, low voices.

But John did not give up so easily. "Don't you want to learn to fight and defend yourself? It's dangerous out there, you know!"

Samson shook his head in disagreement. "Kung-fu isn't for fighting," he said. "It's for training your mind and your body. It's not for killing or hurting."

"Bull!" burst out Winston. "You're just chicken. You're afraid to fight, that's all."

John felt a chill cut through him as he sensed he had started something that was getting out of hand. Samson glanced at Winston for a second, then, ignoring him, turned and addressed John again. "We figure that we've lost three games because of you. Two you didn't show up for, and one last week you were late for. Our points are way down!"

"Stop nagging," interjected Winston. "Who do you think you are, his mother?"

"Who do *you* think you are?" retorted Samson. "His bodyguard?"

"Maybe I am." Winston drew himself up and pushed his chest out. "I protect my friends, especially from goons like you." And he gave Samson a push in the chest. All the kids could see that Winston was spoiling for a fight.

John wanted to cry out, "Stop it! You guys can't fight. You're not enemies, you're my friends!"

But Samson was looking at John. "Can you bring the shinpads and stuff back soon? We need the equipment for practice."

"Leave him alone!" threatened Winston. He reached for Samson again but Samson turned slightly, seized Winston's right wrist with one hand and thrust the other down at Winston's elbow. His arm was snapped straight and Samson forced him to bend to the waist. Samson held him there for a moment before releasing him.

"Leave us alone," Samson said quietly. "We have other things to do."

Winston recovered and stalked away. The Dragons turned back to their game. John stood there for a moment, feeling miserable and confused. Then he ran after Winston, who was heading back to the studio.

"Are you okay?"

Winston nodded, but his stony face did not show any emotion. Just like the heroes in the movies, thought John. If they lost a fight, they never showed their anger. Only the bad guys were sore losers. "He's good, that friend of yours," Winston commented carefully. "That was a good move he pulled on me. Want to try it out?"

John agreed, but only because he felt that he owed Winston a favour. At the studio, they took off their jackets and went out on the floor. They started slowly, trying to figure out the exact moves. There had to be a side shift and a wrist hold. Soon Winston thought he had it. He showed it to John and then said, "Let me try it on you. You attack."

John did, and Winston tried the move on him. When John went down, his shoulder jerked painfully. Then John tried it, but Winston corrected him and told him to use more strength in his left arm. They tried it again and again, alternating the attack each time. Winston's twists became faster and harder. John wanted to protest, but was afraid to be called a weakling. His shoulder began to throb from all the yanking.

Then John decided that he would use more muscle too. When Winston came at him, he grabbed the left wrist, twisted it and shoved down at the elbow with all his strength. Winston jerked forward, lost his balance, and shouted in pain when he hit the floor. Mr. Lim came running over.

Winston's face was contorted in pain, and his arm stuck out awkwardly. Mr. Lim gingerly examined Winston's shoulder and arm and then massaged them slowly. John prayed desperately that nothing was broken. He knew he would be in trouble if his parents found out. John was sick with worry and he felt that he had committed another stupid blunder, all on his own, as usual. "Are you okay?" he asked, when Mr. Lim and Winston finally got to their feet. Winston turned away. "Go away. Just leave me alone."

That night John lay in bed for a long time before he fell asleep. Then he had one of his movie dreams. He was a swordsman, slashing with a long sword as he raced around looking for an escape route out of the dungeon he was trapped in. In his haste, he didn't stop to see whose blood he was drawing. When he looked around, the pained faces of Sharon and Samson stared back at him. "I didn't mean to … " he shouted. He awoke with a start and found himself sweating all over.

For the next week, John tried to forget all about kung-fu. He ran home from school each day. He borrowed a huge stack of books from the library. He did his homework religiously, including work that he didn't have to do. On Saturday, when his mother asked why he wasn't at kung-fu class, John lied and said that the classes were all over. He was miserable and lonely, and he was sure he didn't have any friends left in the world. And it was all his own fault.

By Sunday, he had already completed all his chores. He hung around trying to be helpful, but his mother ordered him out so that she could wax the floor. John wandered slowly over to the school, carrying sticks and pads he had to return to the Dragons. He had postponed it long enough, and sooner or later he had to face his former friends. Samson was right, he thought, and he was stupid. He really didn't know what kung-fu was all about. He had rushed into it like a fool.

When he slipped into the courtyard, he wanted to drop the stuff and run, but Samson saw him, and called out, "Hey, I hear you almost put Winston in the hospital!"

"What a fighter! What a man!" cried the others, half jokingly and half admiringly.

"You'll be in the movies soon," someone else said.

John's face fell. "But I didn't mean to. It was an accident. It was dangerous ..." He shook his head sadly and stared at the ground.

"Is the big shot still practising?" asked Samson.

"Yeah, he's back at it," answered John. "He's still trying to figure out that move of yours. That's what we were doing when he got hurt."

"Serves him right," declared Sharon. And the others agreed noisily.

Then John burst out, "But I've quit that class. I hate kung-fu! I wish I'd never started it."

The Dragons grew silent. "You were right, Samson," continued John in a small voice. "I did it all wrong." He fought to hold his tears back but thought, At least I'm not afraid to admit I'm wrong.

Suddenly Sharon screamed, "Watch out!"

John looked up and saw with a gasp that Samson had raised his hockey stick and was bringing it down at him like an axe. Instantly he stepped into the swing of the stick, raising one arm to deflect the stick. Then both hands grabbed the stick and pulled as he kicked out at Samson, forcing him to let go.

John stared at Samson blankly. What was going on? Why would Samson want to bash him in the head? Was he dreaming or had Samson gone crazy? Everyone's eyes were wide open in surprise. What next?

But Samson was grinning. "See? Kung-fu's not all bad. You can take care of yourself now, right? That's all kung-fu should do — train the body to move as fast as the mind thinks."

"Yeah," said Sharon, who quickly caught on. "It's like having a good wrist shot. You've got to be fast, but you have to practise to get control. You want to put the puck in the net, not in the goalie's face, right?"

That's right, John realized. He hadn't ducked backwards from Samson's stick. Now he wouldn't be afraid to face a fast-shooting forward! But then, he had already quit the team, he remembered.

"Kung-fu's just like any other sport," offered Cam. "It gives you good reflexes. You were just as fast as Samson!"

"Hey, sounds like I ought to learn kung-fu!" said Chris. "Then I can make it into the NHL!"

"Sure," said Sharon. "The league needs women players! And when you retire we can make some kung-fu movies! Starring Samson Wong, John Chin, and Christine Thomas!"

There was laughter all around. Then Ray, who had been really impressed by John's quick move, spoke up. "Maybe it's not such a bad idea to learn some kung-fu. Do you really think it would make us a better team?"

"Sure," John cried out. "It's just like a different kind of warm-up exercise!"

After the excited round of chattering about the new plans had died down, Samson put the last word in. "You know what I say about kung-fu? 'Never fight, but never be afraid to fight.' " He looked at John. "Now put on your mask and get in front of that net. We need someone good there!"

And as the Dragons scampered to get into position, Samson whispered to John, "We were really worried when you dropped out. We thought we'd never find a goalie good enough for us!"

Strathcona
Soccer Stars

Strathcona Soccer Stars

CHRISTINE Thomas had not heard such good news in a long time. She felt like jumping up and shouting, *"Wowee!"* to the whole world. But instead, she forced herself to stay cool and calm. Chris did not want to look like a four-year-old at the circus. Now she could hear the boys baiting the girls into a fight as they jeered at the announcement.

Sharon's indignant voice was growing louder and louder at the front of the classroom. "They can so!" she insisted.

"They can not!" sneered Samson.

"Can so!" Sharon rung back angrily. A few girls spoke up to support her.

"Oh, stop pretending!" ordered Samson. He was sitting atop his desk and looking over the class like a little general. "Girls can't play soccer. You guys can't even kick the ball straight!" All the boys laughed in agreement.

Chris stretched out her long legs and leaned further back in her seat. She had heard all these arguments before and had concluded that they accomplished little. But Sharon liked to argue, although sometimes Chris thought that she did it just to impress Ms. Davies. Most of the Asian kids liked to do that.

The announcement had been short, but it had yanked Chris wide awake. The Mainland Women's Soccer League was sponsoring a girls' soccer camp near Squamish out in the mountains north of Vancouver. For two solid weeks, the girls would stay in chalets, jog along mountain trails, swim, and learn soccer. The tryouts for the camp were two weeks away, and the sign-up list lay on Ms. Davies' desk.

Even more exciting was the news that Davidson Ray and Danny Mazzini from the Vancouver Whitecaps soccer team would be guest coaches at the summer camp. Chris almost fell off her chair when she heard that. Davidson was the top forward in the league, and Danny had a dazzling smile that matched his speed. Both of their portraits were already tacked on the wall in Chris's room at home.

Instantly, Chris wanted to go. She would skim across the field and through the other girls like a knife cutting through soft butter. She would become the star of the entire camp. "Who is that girl?" Danny and Davidson would ask as their mouths fell open in amazement. "Where'd a kid from Strathcona learn to play soccer like that?"

Meanwhile, at the front of the classroom, Sharon was fighting a losing battle with the boys.

"Yeah, so how come there isn't a women's pro team, huh?"

Sharon had no ready reply, and the boys began to answer their own question for her.

"Because they don't know the rules!"

"They're scared of the ball!"

"Remember that time when Sharon kicked the ball in and scored for the other team?" Samson reminded them. The classroom was swallowed up in loud laughter while Sharon's face turned red as a tomato.

"Girls can play," Chris heard herself state in a low voice. "They just don't practise enough."

The laughing stopped abruptly. The kids were not used to hearing Chris's voice in class. She was usually silent and distant in her back-row seat, so people assumed that she hated discussions. But now, even Ms. Davies was listening. She encouraged her students to argue in class because she firmly believed it was healthy to speak out.

"No way, Chris," challenged Samson. "When you girls play, the ball goes way over to the next field! It's like you want to play two games!"

Chris tightened her lips and fell silent again. She knew he was right. In physical education class, when the girls played soccer, the ball would get chased sideways somehow, and never move towards either goal mouth. And the boys would be sitting on the side laughing and hooting and yelling for them to "give it up!" Chris wished she had not opened her mouth. She glared at Samson with eyes that could have melted steel.

"So what? There's lots of things girls can do that boys can't," Sharon piped up helpfully.

"But we don't want to run like you girls," laughed David Mitchell. "You run like a bunch of ducks!"

"We didn't say boys could do everything," added Quang. "Girls are just lousy soccer players!"

Fortunately at that point the final bell of the afternoon rang. The debate fizzled immediately as everyone scrambled to clean up. It was Friday, and a bright and sunny weekend lay ahead. Sharon went up to Ms. Davies' desk to sign up, and then she looked back at Chris. She nodded, so Sharon added her name to the list.

"Stupid boys! I hate them!" cried Sharon as they burst through the big doors downstairs. Chris and Sharon paused against the railing and scanned the busy courtyard. It was filled with kids shouting, playing, and chasing around. Clusters of girls formed lines for Chinese skip, while the square ball rinks were crowded with anxious players.

"Yeah," agreed Chris, "but you shouldn't bother with those fights. No one ever wins. It's a waste of time."

"But I can't stand that Samson and his big mouth. He thinks he's so smart!"

"Yeah, but girls *are* crummy players," Chris said. She saw Sharon pull back in surprise at this unusual admission. Then Chris grinned. "But don't worry. It won't be for long. Come on! Let's get a ball and go practise."

"Practise?" Sharon looked dumbfounded. "How? We don't know how to play soccer. That's why we're going to camp."

"Yeah, but first we have to get picked to go," replied Chris. "We've got to make sure we're good enough. Come on!"

Sharon didn't move. "They'll laugh at us," she protested, pointing towards the playing field. Samson and the other boys of the class had grabbed mitts, bats, and a ball on their way out, and now a baseball game was in full swing in the corner of the field.

"Who cares?" Chris shrugged impatiently. "They're all a bunch of jerks anyway." Sometimes Chris really wondered how she and Sharon had ever become friends. She tended to see Sharon as a "good" Chinese kid whose marks and appearance were almost always perfect. Chris, on the other hand, was regarded by most of her teachers as a problem student. Sharon worried if people didn't like her, and she couldn't stand to be laughed at. Chris, however, didn't care what others said about her. It was hockey that had drawn the two girls together. They were the two tallest girls in the class and the most athletically inclined.

"I don't know … " Sharon hesitated. Chris couldn't stand it when Sharon wasted time.

"Let's go," she urged. And when Sharon still did not move, Chris said, "What's the matter? You afraid of the boys?"

"No!" That did the trick. Sharon would never admit to being chicken. The girls ran over to the community centre office and borrowed a ball. Then they headed out to the playing field. Sharon led the way, and took the long way around just to avoid passing by the boys.

111

"Okay, coachie. Here we are." Sharon put the ball down and scowled. She was angry to have been taken somewhere against her will. "What do we do now?" she demanded.

Chris did not know. All she wanted to do was to go to soccer camp. But there was no team around, no whistle, no coach. "Well," she suggested, "why don't we just kick the ball around and see what happens?"

They walked away from each other and began to kick the ball back and forth. The biggest problem for both of them was to stop the ball when it came in really fast. It knocked against their feet and bounced away. They spent more time chasing the ball than kicking it.

"This is no fun," grumbled Sharon, who was painfully aware that the boys were snickering at them.

"What do you want to do, then?" Chris was getting sick of Sharon's unco-operative attitude.

"I don't know! This was your idea!"

"Okay, okay," Chris tried to think fast. "Let's run with the ball. And then you come and try and take the ball away from me."

The girls started on that, but they kicked each other's shins more than the ball.

"Yowch!" Chris suddenly knelt down to roll up the leg of her jeans. She rubbed some comfort into her bruised shin. "Watch what you're doing, dummy!"

"Sorry," muttered Sharon darkly. "You kicked me hard, too, you know."

"Okay, okay," Chris stood up angrily. "Let's try again."

Sharon rolled her eyes towards the sky in annoyance, but Chris ignored her and started dribbling the ball away.

Sharon followed reluctantly, and then, in a spurt of rage, she charged up in a determined effort to take the ball. Chris was surprised at the fierce attack, and tried to push ahead. The next thing she knew, Sharon had tripped over the ball and was flying through the air. She landed heavily in the gravel.

Sharon looked up furiously. The knees of both pant-legs were whitened and ripped. "I hope you're happy. Brand new jeans!"

"That wasn't my fault!" retorted Chris. "You were charging around like a bull!"

"Oh, get lost!" shouted Sharon. She jumped to her feet and ran out of the field.

"Get lost yourself!" Chris frowned at the disappearing figure and swore at her. Then she picked the ball up and headed towards home. If she doesn't want to practise, why'd the dummy go and sign up? Chris thought angrily to herself. If I don't make it to camp, it'll be all her fault! That stupid girl!

When she fell into her bad moods, Chris resented all the Asians that lived around her. It did not matter if they were born here, or if they were from Hong Kong or Vietnam. Normally Chris did not lump them all together into one single bunch of robots who acted and behaved alike, just because of their looks. But sometimes it was too easy to see that the Asian kids were a lot of things that she wasn't — hard-working, obedient, and well-mannered. Chris did not want to be like them. She just wanted to be herself.

But everybody treated her like a lazy troublesome tomboy from the housing project. Often, they took one look at her tangled mop of hair and her dirty jeans and concluded immediately that she was trouble. When Chris walked into the corner drugstore, the cashier's eyes followed her down every aisle as if she were a thief. But now, she thought, if she could go to Squamish, this might all change. People might finally treat her with a little more respect.

When she walked through the door at home, a pleasant surprise was waiting for her. Her dad was visiting!

"Hi, Chris! How's my girl doing?"

"Dad!"

A pair of huge arms wrapped around her and hugged her tightly. And though Chris would never admit it aloud, she liked the way her father smelled, and she clung to him for a second. Mr. Thomas was wearing his usual blue jeans, lumberman's shirt, jean jacket, and work boots. Chris could see a few strands of grey hair cutting through the sides of his head.

Chris's parents had been living apart for three years now. There had been long nights of fighting and yelling between them before the separation. Now they were like friends, although Chris could never be sure how they would treat each other. Sometimes they were cold and distant; at other times, they laughed and relaxed with each other. Mr. Thomas moved around the province to work wherever he could find a job. He had tried everything there was in town: sawmill hand, long-shoreman, swamper, taxi driver, delivery man, and even salesman.

Mrs. Thomas came in with a cup of coffee for her husband. "Your father's going out of town to work," she explained as she sat them all down. "He came to say good-bye."

"What?" Chris glanced at the door and saw the suitcase there for the first time. "But you haven't been here for ages," she wailed. Lately, Chris had felt her father's absence sharply because Mrs. Thomas had been working the night shift in the hotel coffee room. Chris's father was a great storyteller and always had time to listen to Chris. He was definitely better company than the old TV set.

"Where're you going?" Chris asked.

"Up to Merritt. Catching the five o'clock bus."

"When're you coming back?"

"I don't know, honey." Mr. Thomas looked up with such a sad look in his eyes that Chris changed the subject immediately.

"Going to make lots of money?"

Mr. Thomas laughed. "Sure! And I'll be back. You'll get your ten per cent!"

"Is that all?" Chris tried to make him smile. "How about a raise? Haven't you heard about inflation?"

Mr. Thomas sipped the hot coffee thoughtfully. "Do you deserve it? What have you been up to? Any trouble lately?"

"No!" Chris replied emphatically. Then she brightened. "I'm trying to get into a soccer camp out at Squamish!" Excitedly, she poured out all the details about the upcoming tryouts.

"Sounds great," enthused her father. "What do you think, Jean?"

"Another sport?" Mrs. Thomas shook her head. "Chris, when are you ever going to get serious about things?"

"But I am getting serious," insisted Chris. She could always count on her mother to put a damper on things. "That's why I want to go to Squamish. Don't you see? If I don't go, then I'll never learn soccer."

"But why can't you get serious about school?" her mother persisted anxiously. "I don't want you working in a hotel like me when you grow up."

"I won't, Ma!" Chris cried. "I'll be okay."

"She wants to make it in sports, that's all," Mr. Thomas pointed out. "Not all girls want to be doctors or nurses, you know."

"Well, when I was her age, I was working — "

"Oh, we've all heard that one before." Mr. Thomas brushed her aside lightly with a smile. "Hey, Chris, did you know that I used to play soccer in the industrial league?"

"You're kidding!"

"Nope. In fact, that's how your mom and I met. At the athletic grounds." He grinned at Mrs. Thomas. "Isn't that right, Jean?"

Mrs. Thomas smiled in spite of herself, and suddenly, she did not look so tired. "You were the star forward for the warehouse team," she recalled.

"And you always came out onto your front porch to watch. You wore a bright yellow apron, I remember."

Chris's mother pretended to be surprised. "Oh? Shouldn't you have been watching the ball?"

Chris broke in excitedly. "Hey, you've got to coach me, Dad. I need lots of practice!"

"I can't, honey," Mr. Thomas said gently. "I'm catching a bus in an hour — ooops, that's twenty-five minutes. I've got to run!"

He leaped to his feet and checked his pockets for his ticket. When he caught sight of Chris's disappointed face, he went over to her. "Honey, I'm sorry."

"It's okay, Dad," Chris shrugged. She was used to disappointment.

"Hey, I know what you can do." Mr. Thomas's face lit up with a new idea. "Go see my friend Wobby, in the James Apartments. You know where that is, don't you?"

Chris nodded. "Who? Where?"

"Room eight. His name is Wobby, got that?" Mr. Thomas was at the door. "Tell him you're Dave Thomas's daughter and that you need some soccer help, okay?" Then he rushed out the door with his suitcase banging on his knees.

The next morning, Chris woke up feeling nervous and jittery. Her favourite dreams had swum through her head as she slept. Christine Thomas had just won another gold medal. She was the biggest sports star in all of Canada. Her face was on the front page of every magazine, and TV sportscasters rushed to interview her. But Chris brushed it all aside, just to work out. Day after day she would be practising, and nothing could break her concentration. And in the background, there was her mother, smiling and shaking her head. "I never thought she'd make it," she would confess.

After breakfast, Chris went off to see Wobby. The James Apartments had been repaired during the Strathcona Rehabilitation Project. Over ten years ago, the citizens of Strathcona had fought off the city's attempts to bulldoze the neighbourhood. Instead, they persuaded the government to help them repair and upgrade their homes. Now the area was filled with brightly painted houses, neatly repaired fences, and new parks. All kinds of different people were moving into Strathcona. Chris wondered if Wobby was a newcomer like Sharon or a longtime resident like her.

Chris knocked loudly on the door of room number eight. A voice called out, but Chris could not make out the words. She knocked again, and listened hard. The voice called out again, only more loudly. Then the door was flung open, and a clean lemony smell spilled out into the hallway.

"Wot d'ye want?" a gruff voice demanded. A man in jeans and an undershirt stood there. He seemed to be a bit younger than Chris's father, and looked just as strong. But he was not as approachable as Mr. Thomas. He stared warily at Chris.

"Are you Wobby?" Chris asked.

The man nodded. "That's wot they call me."

"I'm Chris. My father is Dave Thomas. He said that I should come and see you."

"He did, did he?" Wobby spoke with an accent and sounded like someone from one of the kooky British comedy shows on TV. "Well, come in, then."

Chris did not know what to think of him. Wobby had not smiled or shown any emotions. He looked her up and down as if she were a sack of fertilizer. She noticed that Wobby walked with a very bad limp. He was careful not to bend his left leg at all.

Then her eyes sprang wide open when she walked into the tiny living room. The top of the TV and the wall shelves were filled with soccer trophies of all sizes and colours. Some were decorated with glittering little statuettes, others had the gleam of polished wood, and there were two or three shiny cups with engravings all along the side. These were all surrounded by team photographs mounted in black frames. Chris rushed over to take a closer look.

"Where are all these teams, anyway?" she finally asked. "I've never heard of them."

"In Britain."

"You were an all-star player!" Chris read. Wobby grunted behind her.

Chris read the lists of names carefully, searching for a familiar one. Many players and coaches in the North American Soccer League teams had come over from Britain. Then she saw a name that she knew. "You played with Terry Wilcox?" she asked in disbelief.

Wobby nodded.

"What was he like?"

"A professional," replied Wobby curtly.

"You even played for Manchester!" Chris exclaimed.

"Just for half a season," Wobby added.

Finally Chris was finished. She turned around and found that Wobby was sitting in his easy chair reading a newspaper. It was as if she were not even there. Not exactly friendly, is he? Chris thought to herself.

"Are you still playing soccer?" she asked.

The newspaper went down slowly. "Your dad didn't tell you?" Wobby sounded surprised. "You mean your dad didn't send you over to pay a sympathy visit?"

"Tell me what? Pay a what visit?" Chris was completely mystified.

Wobby sighed. "You know why my nickname's 'Wobby'? It's short for 'wobbly'. It's my knees. I'm bow-legged. Really badly. A bloodhound could jump between my kneecaps! And running on them gives me a lot of pain. I had to quit playing in Britain, so I came over here. Then I started again in the industrial league. That's where I met your dad. I should've stopped playing a long time before then, but I didn't."

Chris did not ask why, but she could easily guess the answer.

"Too damn proud. Too damn ambitious. Now I can't even walk properly. The doctor says an operation is the only answer, but I told him that I wasn't interested."

Chris started to look down at her own knees to see if she was bow-legged, but Wobby caught her. "Don't worry. You're not. You know, it's funny now. It's the first thing I check when I meet someone. Is he bow-legged?" He shook his head and laughed at himself. "Now let's get down to brass tacks. Why'd Dave send you over?"

Chris quickly told him about the soccer camp at Squamish. But even before she was finished, Wobby was shaking his head disapprovingly.

"Girls don't play soccer," he said. "I don't care how liberated this country thinks it is. Soccer isn't a game for girls."

"You can't say that!" Chris burst out. "Why shouldn't girls play soccer?"

"It's too rough a game. I've seen men hurt badly on the field."

"But it's not as rough as football or hockey," Chris insisted. "You don't have to wear helmets or shoulder pads, or carry a stick."

Wobby remained firm in his position. "Girls back in England don't play," he pointed out.

"But now women are being sent out on the space shuttle!" argued Chris.

"That's because it's safe up there," Wobby answered smugly.

Chris was ready to explode, and she sputtered angrily without saying a word.

"Christine, it's not personal, you know," Wobby continued. "There are certain things that I don't think women should do. Soccer is one of them." He paused and seemed to soften. "Besides, didn't you say the tryouts were two weeks away? That's not enough time to do anything."

Chris stood up stiffly. Anger showed clearly on her face and in the tense thrust of her arms by her sides. "I'd better get going," she announced.

Wobby seemed taken aback by her scowl and abruptness. "You sure are determined to play, aren't you?" he asked.

Chris nodded defiantly.

"Tell you what. You take this book and read it." Wobby limped over to the shelf and pulled out a ragged-looking volume. "This is my old soccer handbook. But stick to the simple stuff, okay?"

Chris accepted the book, but she was not ready to forgive this stubborn male yet. She muttered her thanks and said goodbye.

Chris went home and spent the morning thumbing through Wobby's book. The book had certainly been well used, because the front cover and the first few pages were missing. The pages were all curled at the edges and marked all over in pencil and ink. Typically, the illustrations showed men players only.

When Chris started reading, she was still angry. People like Wobby made her really mad because they didn't listen and they refused to change. And that bothered her because if people didn't change, then housing-project kids would always be regarded as trouble-makers and delinquents, and girls would always be expected to grow up to be nurses and secretaries.

Chris began to feel better as she read further into the book. There were basic hints on how to move the ball, how to head the ball, and how to avoid mistakes. The book showed drills for players to practise, and Chris studied these very carefully. There were exercises to strengthen the legs, for running backwards, for kicking, and for using the head and chest to direct the ball. Gradually Chris became very enthusiastic. "We can do these!" she exclaimed to herself. "They're not hard at all!"

Then she remembered how Sharon had left the field in a huff yesterday. Most of the drills needed at least two players to make the practice effective. Chris sighed and cursed her friend. She wondered if Sharon was still angry. It wasn't my fault that she tripped, Chris thought. Why should I go and say I'm sorry?

Chris was not one for apologising. If people did not like her behaviour, then that was too bad for them. Chris had become used to being a loner. But this time it was different. Chris really wanted to go to soccer camp. She had to show her mother that she was serious about sports. She had to show people like Samson and Wobby that they were wrong about girls. And she had to prove that she could be a winner too.

A little while later, Chris was knocking on the door of the co-op unit where the Fong family lived. Sharon opened the door, but did not say a word.

"Hi," Chris started. "Want to play soccer?"

Sharon looked blankly at her. "Like yesterday? No, thanks!"

"Oh, no." Chris hurried to reassure her. "Not like yesterday. Are your knees okay?" Chris peered downward to see if Sharon was bow-legged.

"Yeah, they're fine," Sharon responded. "They're just scratched up."

"Anyway," continued Chris awkwardly, holding up Wobby's gift, "I've got this handbook that tells you everything you need to know to play soccer. I've been reading it, see?"

126

Sharon looked at it doubtfully. "Soccer from a book?"

"Sure! It's just like a cookbook! You read the instructions and away you go. Come on! You want to try?"

Sharon looked down and kicked at her toes. "I guess so," she finally said.

Then Chris took a deep breath and said something that she rarely did. "I'm sorry about yesterday, Sharon. Maybe I pushed too hard."

Sharon stared at her in surprise. "Well, I'm sorry too. I guess I was in a bad mood. I'll go put on my shoes."

Chris turned, sat down on the doorstep, and sighed with relief. It was not so painful to apologise, after all. She felt as if a great load had been lifted from her shoulders. Then she nipped through the handbook to check on the drills she wanted to try as soon as they reached the playing field.

A week and a half later, Chris and Sharon were still on the field playing soccer. They had been practising every day after school before Sharon had to go to Chinese school. It was amazing what a few instructions could do. They learned how to use the side of one foot to push the ball when they passed it; and how to point with the other foot.

Chris learned to keep her head up, to look around, and to follow through with her kicking leg. Chris felt a new sense of power and control rise inside her as the ball obeyed her every wish.

The girls were enjoying themselves. Sharon had taken Wobby's book home to read, and she, too, had come back feeling inspired. Today, they were trying something called the five-step drill. As soon as one person passed the ball, she would quickly move five steps away and be ready for the ball. Kick, then move. Stop the ball, look for your partner, and then send the ball over. The girls played faster and faster; they were concentrating so hard that they did not notice that Samson, David Mitchell, and Quang had come up to watch them.

Suddenly, with a loud shout, David burst between the girls and made off with the soccer ball. Samson and Quang followed him, and they began to pass the ball between the three of them as if they owned it.

"Hey, come back here!" shouted Chris. She swore angrily at the boys' interference. The boys ignored her and moved the ball down to the second set of goal mouths. Chris and Sharon set off in hot pursuit, determined to recover their ball. David was dribbling the ball casually and thumbing his nose at the girls. Just as the girls ran up to him, he deftly passed the ball over to Samson.

It happened over and over. The girls went after the ball but as soon as they came up to it, whoever had it would send it beyond their reach.

"Come on, can't you get the ball?" jeered David.

"You guys have been practising all week! You can do better!"

"Over here! Over here!" they taunted.

Chris was getting angrier and angrier. They should never have chased the boys, she realized. She and Sharon had fallen into the boys' trap. Now they had to play the game as the boys directed.

Suddenly a familiar voice called out to Chris. "Stop your senseless chasing, Christine. Get between the boys. And watch the ball!"

It was Wobby, and he was leaning on the other side of the chain-link fence. Chris stopped in her tracks and moved towards the centre of the triangle formed by the three boys. Then Sharon ran at Quang, who had the ball, and forced him to send it away. Now Chris was in position to time her intercepting move. She quickly passed it back to Sharon and ran off to give herself some running room. In a second, Sharon had sent the ball flying back to Chris, and she began to drive it back to their field in a rapid dribble as Sharon moved up alongside her.

The boys were speechless with surprise at the quick and sure moves of the girls. Then it was their turn to chase the girls. Chris and Sharon were thrilled with their own moves, for they had done it even under pressure from the boys.

Quang was the fastest runner and he came up quickly beside Chris. She was just about to pass the ball to Sharon when Quang swung his foot across her path trying to tip the ball away. Instead, Chris tripped over his foot and went flying into the gravel. She landed on one knee heavily and a flash of pain shot through her entire leg. Quang's foot was tangled in there somewhere too, and he lost his balance and fell onto the seat of his pants.

Sharon dashed in from the other side and scooped up the ball. Then she turned to Chris, who was sitting up dazedly. There were rips in her jeans at the knees and her palms were bloodied. She shook her head, trying to get rid of the dizziness.

"Are you okay?" Sharon asked worriedly.

Chris grimaced. "Wobby was right," she muttered to herself. "It is a rough game." And to Sharon she said, "Now we're even. One pair of jeans gone to soccer for each of us!"

The boys were standing around looking sheepish.

"You okay, Chris?" Quang asked. "I'm sorry."

"Hey, Chris, you guys aren't bad!" jumped in Samson quickly.

"All that practice is paying off," David added. "You guys should make it into that soccer camp."

Quang and Samson swiftly echoed their agreement to cover up their embarrassment. "Yeah, you guys really deserve to get in."

All this nice-guy talk was making Chris sick. The boys could overdo things when they tried to be sorry. "We're fine, okay?" she said. "Why don't you just leave us alone?"

"Yeah, how about right now!" Sharon said sharply.

The boys saw Wobby approaching and backed off hurriedly. Wobby limped up to the two girls. He shook out his handkerchief and gave it to Chris to mop up her hands. "If there's anything that I don't like," he said gruffly, "its three playing against two."

The girls grinned at him. "Thanks for coming by."

"I was just passing by," Wobby replied. "You girls were doing okay before the boys came along. The old handbook's pretty useful, isn't it?"

"It sure is!" cried Sharon. "Thanks a lot!"

"When are the tryouts?" enquired Wobby.

"This weekend. We've been practising every day."

Chris was trying to stand up, but as soon as she put any weight on her leg, pain shot up through her entire body. Her face was pinched with the momentary pain.

"I told you it was a rough game," chided Wobby.

"I know, I know," replied Chris. She turned to Sharon. "Okay, let's get the ball rolling."

"Do you think you should?" Sharon hesitated and looked anxiously at Chris. "Maybe you ought to rest your leg a bit first."

"Ah, a little pain never hurt an athlete," said Wobby pompously. "It'll be okay once you play on it."

Chris looked uncertainly at her two companions.

"It hurts, right?" Sharon asked.

Chris nodded, and felt a bit scared.

"Then you should rest it," concluded Sharon. "When your body hurts, it's telling you to take it easy. It needs time to fix itself."

Wobby snorted in disgust and stomped off. "I'm going! Good luck!"

"How does it feel?" Sharon asked.

"So-so," Chris replied. "I can walk, see?" She hobbled around for a few steps. "Come on, let's play!"

"No!" Sharon was firm. "I've got to go to Chinese school now anyway. Why don't you take it easy for a while?" Before Chris could say anything, Sharon had run off with the ball.

As she walked slowly home, the pain began to subside. Chris knew that it would be okay in a little while. But strangely enough, she was almost glad that the accident had happened in front of so many witnesses. The boys had made fools of both her and Sharon on the field. The two of them were really not that good at soccer yet. Now she reasoned that if she did not win at the tryouts, she would at least have the sore leg as an excuse.

When Chris walked into the house, Mrs. Thomas came out of the bedroom, dressed in her coffee-shop uniform. She was just about to leave for work. "Oh, look at your pants," she scolded.

"I know, I know." Chris plopped down on the sofa and massaged her knee. It was fine now, but she still stared grimly at it.

Mrs. Thomas detected the drop in Chris's spirits and she sat down for a second. "Are you and Sharon ready for the tryouts?" she asked.

"I don't know," Chris replied in a small voice. "We're not that good." And she told how the boys had humiliated them that afternoon, before Wobby came along.

"Is your knee okay?" Mrs. Thomas asked first.

"It's okay." Chris paused. "Maybe I shouldn't go on Sunday." Chris thought that might make her mom happy.

Mrs. Thomas shook her head in bewilderment. "But why? Don't you want to go to Squamish any more?"

"I don't know," Chris squirmed uncomfortably under her mother's curious gaze. She was not going to admit that maybe she was afraid of losing.

"Well, all you can do is try your best," said Mrs. Thomas finally.

Chris was silent. She stared at her shoes.

Her mother sighed. Sometimes she could not understand her daughter at all. "I have to go now. See you tomorrow!"

Soon the day of the tryouts arrived. It turned out to be a wet, grey day with heavy clouds over-head. Chris and Sharon went to the park on the bus wearing their shorts and windbreakers. Chris had finally decided, after much thought, to go to the tryouts. She had not slept well the night after her talk with her mother.

I'm not really afraid of losing, she said to herself. I'm not a poor sport! It was true, for Chris didn't mind losing in a game that was well played. This time, however, she felt she might lose to girls from the West Side, where kids started earlier in all kinds of sports and where they had real coaches. So if Chris lost today, she knew it would not be because she was a poor player, but because the others had an advantage. But most of the spectators would not know that. They would just see that she wasn't a very good soccer player.

But Chris could not admit defeat without a good try. There was, after all, a slim chance that she would make it to Squamish. The camp was still the chance of a lifetime to see and do a lot of the things that Chris wanted most. Then, too, her mother was right. All she could do was try her hardest. If she didn't go to the tryouts, she would never know how good or bad she was.

There were more than two hundred girls gathered in the park for the selection. They were all given big numbers to wear on their fronts and backs. The panel of judges, who were all women, put the girls through all kinds of drills. They were timed running from one goal line to the other while dribbling a ball. There were obstacle courses to run, passing games, target-shooting, and exercises involving trapping the ball, heading it, and throwing it in from the sidelines.

Many parents and interested guests had come to watch, but Chris did not see anyone she knew. As she watched the other girls go through the tests, she tried not to think too much. Chris could see that there were some very talented girls on the field, and she tried not to let that scare her. On the brighter side, there were some girls who had obviously never been near a soccer ball. Once or twice Chris almost laughed at them, but generally she felt sorry for them.

Chris felt cold and jittery during the whole morning, and kept jumping up and down on her toes to stay warm as she waited for her turn. She and Sharon were both so nervous that they did not say much to each other. Chris tested her injured knee to make sure that it was okay. After the first drill, Chris was warmed up and loosened up, and then she could really concentrate on the tests. She was relieved when all the tests were completed. It was almost noon, and Chris could hear her stomach rumbling. They all waited anxiously for the results.

Then the co-ordinator of the panel stood up on a chair and put the megaphone to her mouth. "The results have been tallied and all the evaluations done. I'll read out the list of girls going to Squamish, in alphabetical order."

Chris sucked in a breath and clenched her hands tightly. This was it! She glanced at Sharon and they smiled weakly at one another. Chris could feel the nervous excitement quivering through the crowd.

The co-ordinator started reading the names. There were happy shouts of joy mingled with groans of disappointment from the girls. Then Chris realized that the list had already reached the Js and Sharon's name had not been called.

Chris could feel herself getting wound up tighter and tighter. Her head began to spin. She didn't want to go if Sharon couldn't go, she thought for a second. But what about Danny and Davidson? And what about showing what housing-project kids could do?

"Stefanelli, Joanie," called the judge, "Thomas, Christine, and Wong, Elaine. And that's everyone. Thank you all for coming. We will all keep in contact."

Then everyone broke out in applause.

"I made it!" exulted Chris. "Wowee!"

"Congratulations!" shouted Sharon, clapping Chris on the back. "You did it!"

Chris nodded, but she was confused. She had made it, but now she felt she was losing her friend. Was this supposed to happen?

"Come on, lets go eat!" said Sharon. "Don't worry about me. I'm not going to sit and moan and groan about it." She was cheerful already. "You're the best person to go. You'll show everyone that kids from Strath are dynamite too!"

But despite Sharon's encouraging words, Chris could feel her disappointment. She looked at Sharon and felt that somehow she had hurt her friend. But she hadn't done anything. Why did there always have to be winners and losers? Why couldn't they both have gone to soccer camp?

"Remember to come back, eh!" teased Sharon. "Don't let super-stardom go to your head!"

"Of course I'll come back," replied Chris. Finally things were falling into place. "And then we're going to start the best girls' soccer team in the whole city right at home!"

Afterword

Beginnings, and New Beginnings

Strathcona is one of Vancouver's very special neighbourhoods, and one of its oldest. Many Chinese Canadian families, like Sharon's, John's, and Samson's, live there together with people from other Asian and European backgrounds.

Strathcona is located adjacent to Chinatown, where Sharon's grandfather lives, and close to downtown Vancouver. The Chinese Canadians who live there possess a rich history and their story is told in the following pages.

Before 1858, the area of Canada that later became British Columbia was the home of the Native Indians. They hunted and fished throughout the area. British Columbia was one of the last parts of North America to be claimed by the Europeans.

In 1858, gold was discovered, and men from around the world poured into British Columbia. The Chinese arrived at this time, first from California and then from China itself. In the scramble for gold, the Chinese miners were not always welcomed by whites and they were often beaten, robbed, and even murdered.

142

Men working in a salmon cannery. About 1890.
(Vancouver City Archives 196-1)

The Chinese had come to Canada, like immigrants from other countries, to look for work. In China, the over-crowded land could no longer feed the growing population. Almost all of the Chinese immigrants came from a small area near the cities of Hong Kong and Canton. Men left their families at home and sent money back to them whenever they could. This was a practice common among European immigrants in North America, too.

During the gold rush, the Chinese worked at many different jobs. They started laundries, restau-

Men building the railway through the mountains to link British Columbia to the rest of Canada. (Vancouver Public Library no. 1773)

rants, and vegetable farms that served the bachelor white miners. Early industries and new construction projects required many workers. White workers preferred to prospect for gold in hopes of getting rich quickly. Thus Chinese workers were hired to work in coal-mines, salmon canneries, and lumber mills, where they were paid very little. They also built roads and strung telegraph wires.

Many more workers were needed in 1880, when work began on the western section of the Canadian Pacific Railway. Many Chinese immigrants were willing to work hard and were hired. They cleared and graded the pathway where the tracks would be laid. This meant drilling through rocks and mountains. The Chinese back-packed their provisions and equipment and set up camps all along the rail line. Chinese workers were paid one dollar a day — half of a white worker's pay.

Living conditions were unhealthy and the Chinese suffered from sickness and cold. Many of them died during the building of the railway — from illness, rock explosions, tunnel collapses, and drowning. When it was finished in 1885, the remaining workers were left to fend for themselves. Some moved east through the Rockies, some settled in towns along the rail line, and others headed to Victoria and the new city of Vancouver to look for work.

In towns and cities with large Chinese populations, unfriendly white attitudes caused the Chinese to group together in neighbourhoods called Chinatowns. These areas contained the stores, homes, hostels, and association halls of the Chinese.

In the large Chinatowns, such as those in Vancouver and Victoria, the Chinese formed organizations to help each other. They helped people find jobs, housing, and friends. They also took care of the poor and the sick, and fought against the unfair treatment of the Chinese.

From the earliest days, white British Columbians had disliked the Chinese because they were different, in both looks and customs. As more Chinese arrived, anti-Chinese feelings grew worse. White workers feared losing their jobs to the Chinese. Politicians and journalists said the Chinese could never assimilate into Canadian life. They wanted Chinese immigration stopped.

Laws that discriminated against the Chinese were passed in the 1870s. The Chinese were not allowed to vote and so they had no voice in government. Every Chinese person entering Canada had to pay a tax, which no other immigrants had to pay. It was hoped that these laws would keep Chinese from coming here. But men like Skyfighter and Sharon's grandfather paid the tax and came anyway.

In Vancouver, there was a group of people who tried, illegally, to drive the Chinese out of the city. A crew of Chinese land-clearers was forced out, but they did not give up and came back to the city. Later, another Chinese camp was attacked and burned, and all the Chinese in town were loaded onto wagons and sent out of town. A special police force was sent to the city to stop the violence. The Chinese then returned and settled back into their jobs and lives in the city.

At the mills they cut logs and packed the shingles. Others dug ditches, built dikes, and cleared the forest. Many became farmers, supply-

A merchant tailor's shop where seamsters made clothing for local citizens. About 1900. (Dr. Wallace Chung)

ing fresh produce to the growing city. Most of them had come from farms in China and possessed valuable agricultural skills, which they used very successfully. The Chinese were cooks and servants too, working in hotels, in logging camps, on ships, and in white families' homes.

Vancouver's Chinatown had its own thriving economy at this time, which provided many jobs. Clerks, bookkeepers, and shippers worked for companies that shipped food and other goods from China to the interior of British Columbia. Tailors

A corner grocery shop owned and operated by a Chinese grocer. Such stores existed all over Vancouver and often stayed open late at night for the convenience of their customers. About 1920. (Vancouver Public Library no. 7921)

who made workmen's pants, overalls, and boys' clothing set up businesses and hired many seamsters.

The merchants of Vancouver brought their wives over from China and raised families here. Their children attended school with other children in Vancouver; some were tutored in Chinese at home, or sent back to China for a Chinese education. These children spoke English and Chinese equally well.

As the population in Vancouver increased, living conditions in Chinatown became very crowded. Dormitories were run by Chinese associations for bachelor men, and merchant families lived behind or above their stores. Some families lived in Strathcona, just east of Chinatown. A few Chinese families moved into white neighbourhoods, but they were isolated. Chinatown was the centre of the community, where the Chinese felt safe and comfortable.

As more Chinese came to Canada, feeling against them increased. In September of 1907, a mob of three thousand whites rioted through Chinatown. In 1923, the Canadian government banned Chinese immigration. That meant that no more Chinese could come into Canada and that men already living in Canada could not send for their families to join them. Soon the Chinese population began to drop.

The future for young Chinese Canadians growing up at this time did not look bright. They could not find jobs except in Chinatown or in family businesses, even though they spoke English and had university degrees. Nevertheless, this Canadian-born generation of Chinese remained proud and active. They formed a championship soccer team and organized clubs for tennis, swimming, and flying.

This photograph shows the arch of jade and bamboo that the Chinese built to celebrate Vancouver's fiftieth birthday. 1936. (Vancouver Public Library no. 41)

The older generation of Chinese pioneers shrank as they died of old age, or illnesses resulting from malnutrition and poor living and working conditions. Some returned to China; others could not afford a ticket to go home. These people turned for help to the Chinatown associations that they belonged to.

However, during the depression, attitudes toward the Chinese began — slowly — to change. They still suffered from discrimination. For example, unemployed Chinese did not get equal treatment from the government when food and bed tickets were given out. But white workers were gradually coming to the realization that the fight to help the unemployed would never be successful unless *all* of B.C.'s workers were prepared to pull together. They began to try to help the Chinese deal with the difficulties they and white workers shared. In 1936, the Chinese even helped celebrate Vancouver's fiftieth birthday by staging a huge festival. They built an arch of jade and bamboo, and invited the whole city to join in the celebrations.

The Second World War drastically changed whites' attitudes towards the Chinese. At the beginning of the war, Chinese Canadians were not conscripted into the army, even though soldiers were badly needed. Politicians were afraid that the government would have to give the Chinese full citizenship rights if they died fighting for Canada.

But young Chinese-Canadian volunteers still joined the army and went to fight in Europe and Asia. At home in Canada, Chinese Canadians worked in new fields. The war had created a labour shortage and a demand for war supplies. Workers were needed for local war industries such as ship-building and aircraft construction.

After the war, standards of living rose across the country because more work and higher wages were available. The Chinese in British Columbia were given the right to vote and laws were changed to allow Chinese families to be reunited. Sharon's father belonged to a generation of sons and daughters who came over to join their fathers. These young people learned English, found work, and started families.

With the Chinese coming into Canada once again, Vancouver's Chinese community began to grow. Many families moved into Strathcona. It was close to Chinatown and housing costs were low. Italians, Portuguese, Scandinavians, and Eastern Europeans had already made their homes there.

Through these years, more job and housing opportunities opened up for the Chinese. Families started to move into different areas of the city. They no longer relied on Chinatown for jobs or housing.

These members of a martial arts school join in the festivities around the Chinese New Year's parade in Vancouver, 1980. (Jim Wong-Chu)

Soon many Canadian-born Chinese were growing up without learning Chinese or feeling any attachment to Chinatown.

Yet, when it seemed that Chinatown and Strathcona might be destroyed to be replaced by public housing and freeways, groups of Chinese Canadians joined the fight to save both these neighbourhoods. The public housing was built anyway, and so families like Christine Thomas's moved into Strathcona. New parks, roads, and a community centre were also constructed.

Since 1967, the number of Chinese in Vancouver has risen dramatically and this has given Chinatown a new vitality. Recent immigrants from Hong Kong have started bakeries, stereo stores, jewellery stores, and restaurants. Chinatown has overflowed its old boundaries in order to meet the demand for new foods and new community services.

Vancouver's Chinese population includes many different kinds of Chinese people. The older bachelor men like Skyfighter and Sharon's grandfather stay close to Chinatown. There are Canadian-born Chinese like Sharon and her mom who speak more English than Chinese. The majority do not live in Strathcona and have little to do with Chinatown. But they still have to think about what it means to be Chinese-Canadian in today's multicultural society.

John and Samson's families represent another part of the Chinese community. They are the newcomers from Hong Kong, Taiwan, China, and many other parts of the world. They include many professional people and wealthy families who do not choose to live in Strathcona. But there are also new immigrants with working-class and rural backgrounds. And lately, refugees from Vietnam have also settled in Strathcona. Social service agencies work with those who need help in language and in adjustment.

Chinatown today means different things to the various Chinese people living in Vancouver. New immigrants see it as a comfortable place to work and shop. Others see it as the centre of the Chinese community, where activities promote Chinese and Chinese-Canadian culture. Some go there just for the excellent restaurants.

Strathcona is a residential neighbourhood, while Chinatown is a commercial and cultural centre. Both have taken on a new importance to all of Vancouver and are recognized as historically and culturally important parts of the city. They are full of exciting memories and challenging opportunities for the future.